LIES FOR LOVE

Suddenly and unexpectedly, there was the sound of the bolt being raised on the door, and Carmela sat up, alert and half-fearful that it might be Matthews or Lane returning. Then as the sunlight flooded in she saw the outline of a man, large and broad-shouldered, silhouetted against the trees outside, and she gave a cry of joy.

Then the Earl was beside her, pulling her into his arms.

She held on to him, saying incoherently, her words falling over one another: "You have . . . found . . . me! I . . . prayed that . . . you would . . . come! I was . . . so afraid . . . that I would . . . die before . . . you did."

"I have found you," the Earl said.

Then as tears of relief ran down Carmela's cheeks, his lips came down on hers and he held her mouth captive. . . .

Bantam Books By Barbara Cartland
Ask you bookseller for the books you have missed

About Barbara Cartland
 CRUSADER IN PINK

Lies for Love

Barbara Cartland

BANTAM BOOKS
TORONTO · NEW YORK · LONDON · SYDNEY

LIES FOR LOVE
A Bantam Book / March 1982

ISBN 0-553-20747-4

Published simultaneously in the United States and Canada

Bantam Books are published by Bantam Books, Inc. Its trade-
mark, consisting of the words "Bantam Books" and the por-
trayal of a rooster, is Registered in U.S. Patent and Trademark
Office and in other countries. Marca Registrada. Bantam
Books, Inc., 666 Fifth Avenue, New York, New York 10103.

Author's Note

At the beginning of the Nineteenth Century the penalty for robbery of any sort was very severe. A person was hanged for "privately stealing in a shop, warehouse and coachhouse or stable to the amount of five shillings."

Poaching a hare or a pheasant meant, as a merciful sentence, transportation in a convict ship to New South Wales for seven years.

The prisons were filthy shambles, the police were inadequate, badly organised, and poorly paid, which meant they were often corrupt.

A boy arrested for minor pilfering could be sent to prison, flogged, then turned out without a penny in his pocket.

Select Committees set up in 1817 produced numerous petitions to Parliament, but the Reform Bill was many frustrating years ahead.

Lies for Love

Chapter One

"Henry, stop kicking Lucy and eat up your porridge," Carmela said.

"I won't!"

Henry was a fat, ugly boy nearly seven years of age
and in Carmela's opinion was quite uncontrollable.

To prove his defiance he gave his sister Lucy
another kick, and she started to cry.

"Stop that at once, do you hear?" Carmela said
sharply, thinking as she spoke that it would have little
effect.

She was right.

Henry picked up his bowl of porridge and deliberately turned it upside-down on the table-cloth.

At the same time the baby in the cot, awakened by
the noise Lucy was making, started to cry too.

Carmela thought helplessly that there was really
nothing she could do about them.

It was almost to be expected, she thought, as she
had thought many times since she came to the Vicarage, that the Vicar's children should be the worst
behaved and most unmanageable of any in the village.

Because she felt she could do nothing with Henry,
and Lucy would cry whatever happened, she went to
the cot to pick up the baby and rock him in her arms.

As she was doing so the door opened and the
Vicar's wife put her head round it to say:

"Can't you keep those children quiet? You know the Vicar's trying to write his sermon for tomorrow."

"I am sorry, Mrs. Cooper," Carmela apologised.

The Vicar's wife did not wait for her answer but merely shut the door so sharply that it sounded suspiciously like a slam.

Henry waited until his mother had gone, then shouted above the noise his sister was making:

"I want my egg!"

"You can have it after you have eaten your porridge," Carmela replied.

She knew as she spoke that she was fighting a losing battle.

Sure enough, while she was away from the table Henry seized the egg-cup next to the ones intended for his sister and Carmela, and after knocking off the top of the egg started to eat it eagerly.

Carmela felt desparingly that there was nothing she could do with him.

Ever since she had come to the Vicarage to look after the children she had known that however clever she might be, she could not control Henry.

His parents must have discovered how difficult he was almost as soon as he was born. They had given in to him on every occasion and allowed him to have his own way, with the result that like a cuckoo in the nest he pushed the other children aside and invariably got what he wanted.

Sometimes when she went to bed at night too tired to sleep, Carmela thought she could not face the years ahead spent in looking after children like Henry and knowing that she was capable of making little or no impact on them.

After her father died there had been the necessity of finding herself employment of some sort, and when Mrs. Cooper suggested that she come to the Vicarage it had seemed the easy solution to her problem.

She told herself that at least she would be staying

amongst people whom she knew and who did not make her afraid.

She faced her position bravely and admitted that she was afraid of being alone, afraid of going out into an alien, hostile world, and most of all, afraid of being incompetent.

That her father had always found her very intelligent was quite a different thing from being able to earn money by using her brain.

Her father had tried to do so by selling his pictures, which unfortunately had not proved at all saleable.

Just occasionally he received what seemed to Carmela and her mother a large sum for a portrait of some local dignitary, but the pictures he really enjoyed painting were on the whole "too beautiful to be sold."

That was how her mother had once described them, and they had all laughed, but Carmela had known exactly what she meant and why her father's pictures did not appeal to the ordinary purchaser.

But to her the manner in which he painted the mist rising over a stream at dawn, or a sunset behind distant hills, was so lovely that she felt as if when she looked at them they carried her into a mystical world which only she and her father realised existed.

It was the same world she had known as a child when he had told her stories of fairies and goblins, of elves and nymphs, and showed her the mushroom-rings in the fields where the "little people" had danced the night before.

It was a world of wonder and beauty and to Carmela it was very real, but it was not really something one could express on canvass. Peregrine Lyndon's beautiful pictures therefore stayed in the Art Dealer's shop until he sent them back as unsaleable.

Her mother had died first, and there was very little money coming into the small house where they lived on the edge of the village.

This was because the only way Carmela's father

could assuage his grief was by painting the pictures that appealed to him, and he gave up suggesting to the fat Aldermen in the market-town five miles away, and the local Squires, that they should have their portraits painted.

Because her father was so handsome and what in the village they called a "perfect gentleman," it was locally considered a compliment to be painted by him.

Unfortunately, however, few people in Huntingdon were willing to pay for such luxuries and therefore Peregrine Lyndon's commissions were few and far between.

The house became filled with the pictures he liked to paint, and after her mother's death Carmela would ask her father when the day was over what work he had done, to find as often as not that because it dissatisfied him he had cleaned off his canvass and started again.

"I always think of your mother," he would say, "when I see the sun rising above the horizon."

In consequence he expected each picture to be perfection, and he would paint the same scene over and over again but still not be satisfied with the result.

Only by taking the canvasses away from him after two or three attempts could Carmela keep the pictures she liked best from being destroyed. She had to hide them in her bedroom to look at them when she was alone.

When her father died last winter, having caught pneumonia through sitting out in the bitter cold and frost to paint the stars, as soon as she could take in what had happened she had discovered that all she possessed in the world were her father's pictures, which nobody wanted, and the few pounds which was all she could get by selling the contents of the house.

The house itself was only rented, and although what they paid was very little she knew that she could not find even that amount without earning it.

It was when she was in the depths of despair over losing her father, whom she had dearly loved, that Mrs.

Cooper's suggestion that she might work at the Vicarage had seemed like a glimmer of light in the darkness.

It was only when she had moved in to the ugly house and was confronted by the Vicar's extremely plain children that she realised to what misery she had committed herself.

But she could think of nothing else she could do, and at least the Vicarage would provide a roof over her head and food to eat that she did not have to pay for.

With some embarrassment Mrs. Cooper had suggested she should pay her ten pounds a year for her labours, and as Carmela had no idea if that was generous or not, she had accepted the offer thankfully.

Now she thought, as she had a dozen times already, that she would rather starve than go on trying to cope with children whose only response to everything she said was to be rude and obstructive.

Carmela had always thought that anyone with any intelligence should be able to communicate with other human beings, however primitive or difficult they might be.

She had often talked with her father of the way Missionaries travelled in countries inhabited by savage tribes and somehow gained their confidence even though in many cases they could not speak their language.

"Men and women should be able to communicate with one another in the same way as animals do," Peregrine Lyndon had said.

He had therefore believed that there must be people somewhere in the world who would understand what he was trying to say on canvass because it was something which came from both his mind and his heart.

"I think the truth is that you are in advance of your time, Papa," Carmela had told him. "Artists at the moment want to portray exactly what they see. In the past there have been men like Botticelli and Michelangelo, who painted with their imagination, and that is what you are trying to do."

"I am honoured by the company in which you include me," her father had said with a smile. "But you are right. I want to put down what I think and feel, rather than what I actually see with my eyes, and as long as you and I understand, why should we worry about anybody else?"

"Why indeed?" Carmela had replied.,

However, imagination did not pay the butcher, the baker, or the grocer, and their Landlord would not accept "imaginary" money.

The baby stopped crying and fell asleep, and Carmela laid him down very gently in his cot. At the moment he was comparatively good, but she felt that he would soon grow up to be like his brother and sister.

As she turned towards the table, Lucy gave a little scream.

"Henry's eating my egg! Stop him, Miss Lyndon! He eating my egg!"

It was true, Carmela saw. Henry, having eaten his own egg, had now taken the brown one which was set on one side for Lucy.

This too he was eating as quickly as he could, defying her with his small pig-like eyes to stop him.

"Never mind, Lucy," Carmela said to the small girl, "you can have my egg."

"I want mine, it's brown!" Lucy expostulated fiercely. "I hate Henry, I hate him! He's always taking my things!"

Carmela looked at Henry and thought she hated him too.

In front of him on the table the porridge was oozing out from the bowl, which had cracked when he turned it over.

The empty egg-shell from the first egg had fallen out of the egg-cup, and the yoke from the second egg was spilling onto the table-cloth because of the haste in which he was eating it.

It was also spattered on his white shirt, which

Carmela had spent a long time yesterday washing and pressing.

She did not say anything but merely put her egg in front of Lucy, took the top off it, and put a clean spoon in her hand.

"I want a brown egg—a brown one!" Lucy shrieked. "I don't like white ones!"

"They taste exactly the same inside," Carmela tried to console her.

"You're a liar!" Henry said rudely.

"That's right! You're a liar!" Lucy echoed, forgetting her anger with her brother and glad to have an ally against a common enemy. "Brown eggs taste different from white ones! I want a brown egg!"

Carmela gave a sigh and sat down at the table.

She filled her cup with the cheap, rather unpleasant-tasting tea which was all that was provided at the Vicarage and cut herself a slice of bread from a loaf which had been stale yesterday.

Lucy was still screaming for a brown egg when suddenly, getting into a worse tantrum than she was in already, she hit the egg in front of her with the back of her hand.

It shot across the table and smashed against the teapot. The yoke spattered in all directions and Carmela received a large portion of it on her hand.

She opened her lips to reprove Lucy, then suddenly thought the whole thing was too much for her.

She felt the tears come into her eyes, and as she did so the door behind her opened.

She stiffened, expecting to hear Mrs. Cooper's querulous voice demanding that she should keep the children quiet, or else the Vicar shouting at them, which always made things worse.

Then when she was aware that somebody had come into the room but had not spoken, she turned her head.

Then she stared in astonishment.

Standing in the doorway, making the untidy room

that was used as a Nursery look even more unpleasant than it usually did, was a Vision of loveliness.

The Vision wore a high-crowned bonnet trimmed with flowers and a high-waisted gown of sprigged muslin trimmed with bows of mauve ribbon, and had a very attractive face with two exceedingly large blue eyes and a red mouth, which was smiling at her.

"Hello, Carmela!"

"Felicity!"

Carmela jumped up from the table, wiping the egg-yolk from her hand as she did so, to run to the doorway and kiss the girl who had just appeared.

Lady Felicity Gale was her closest friend, and except when she was away staying with friends, they had been inseparable.

"When did you get back?" Carmela asked. "I have been . . . longing to . . . see you."

Her words seemed to fall over themselves, and Lady Felicity kissed her affectionately as she replied:

"I got back only last night. I could not believe it when I was told you had come to the Vicarage!"

"There was nowhere else I could go after Papa died."

"I had no idea he was dead. Oh, Carmela, I am sorry!"

Carmela did not speak, but she could not help the tears coming into her eyes.

She could be brave until anybody spoke of her father, but then, however hard she tried, it was impossible not to realise how terribly she missed him.

"Now I am back," Lady Felicity said, "and I want you. I want you at once, Carmela!"

"I . . . I am working . . . here."

Lady Felicity looked at the table and the children, who were gaping open-mouthed at her appearance.

"I have something better for you to do than look after these little horrors!" she said. "I remember Henry. He is the one who was always spitting and making faces in Church when his father was not looking."

Carmela laughed. She could not help it.

"Who are you?" Lucy asked, resenting that she was no longer the centre of attention.

"Somebody who is going to take this nice, kind Miss Lyndon away from you," Lady Felicity replied, "and I hope perhaps your father will find somebody horrid to take her place and give you the beating you all deserve!"

She did not sound very ferocious because she was laughing as she spoke. Then, taking Carmela by the hand, she said:

"Get your things. I have a carriage waiting outside."

"But I cannot . . . leave just like . . . that," Carmela protested.

"Yes, you can," Felicity replied, "and while you are packing I will explain to Mrs. Cooper that I need you and it is absolutely essential that you come with me at once."

"She will be furious, Carmela said, "and she will never employ me again!"

"She is not going to have the chance to do so," Felicity stated. "I will explain everything when we get away from here."

She looked round the room and added:

"Hurry, Carmela, I cannot bear to be in such a sordid place longer than a few minutes. I cannot think how you have endured it."

"It has been rather horrid," Carmela admitted, "but, Felicity, I must give my notice in the proper way."

"Leave everything to me," Felicity replied. "Just do as I tell you."

"I . . . I do not think I . . . should."

Even as she spoke Felicity gave her a little push with her kid-gloved hands.

"I need you, I need you desperately, Carmela, and you cannot refuse me."

"I suppose not," Carmela said doubtfully, "and you know I want to come with you, Felicity."

"Then pack your clothes—no, never mind—you will not need them. I have masses of things for you at the Castle."

Carmela looked at her in bewilderment as she went on:

"Just do as I say. Bring only the things you treasure. I expect that includes your father's pictures."

"They are downstairs in an outhouse. There was no room for them here."

"I will tell the footman to collect them," Felicity said, "and then to come upstairs for your trunk. I will go talk to Mrs. Cooper."

Before Carmela could say any more, she turned and left the room.

The children stared after her until Lucy asked:

"Are you going away with that lady?"

"Mama won't let you go," Henry said before Carmela could reply.

It was as if his rude, oafish voice made up her mind for her.

"Yes, I am going away," she said, and ran into the small room next door.

Because there was nowhere else to put her clothes except a small, rickety chest-of-drawers which she shared with Lucy, most of her things had been left packed in her trunk.

She hurriedly packed what she had been using, put the dressing-table set that had been her mother's on top, added a shawl that was on the bed because there were so few blankets, and did up the strap of her trunk.

As she was doing so a footman appeared in the doorway, resplendent in the Gale livery with its crested silver buttons and carrying his cockaded top-hat in his hand.

"Morning, Miss Carmela," he said with a grin.

"Good-morning, Ben."

"Her Ladyship says I were to fetch yer trunk."

"It is there," Carmela said, pointing to where it stood. "Can you manage it alone?"

"Course I can!" Ben replied.

He put his hat on his head, picked up the trunk, and carried it easily across the Nursery.

The children were still sitting at the table, watching what was occurring in astonishment.

As Carmela came from the bedroom wearing the cloak that had belonged to her mother and a plain chip bonnet trimmed with black ribbons, she thought that compared to Felicity she must look like a hedge-sparrow beside a bird-of-paradise.

At the same time, she felt nervous as to what Mrs. Cooper would say.

As she went down the stairs she was aware that the Vicar's wife would have every right to be annoyed and insulted by her precipitate departure.

Carmela had always done whatever Felicity wanted, and although she was in fact only a few months younger in age, at times her friend seemed almost to belong to a different generation.

She had always been the ring-leader in all their activities, and she was also very self-assured, having travelled and met people of importance. She was, Carmela had often said with a smile, in consequence grown-up before she was a child.

As Carmela reached the small dark Hall, she was aware that Felicity was in the Sitting-Room talking to Mrs. Cooper.

With her heart beating apprehensively, Carmela walked into the room half-expecting to receive a torrent of abuse in the querulous voice that Mrs. Cooper could use most effectively when anything annoyed her.

Instead, to her surprise the Vicar's wife was smiling.

"Well, you're a lucky girl, and no mistake!" she said before Carmela could speak. "Her Ladyship's just been telling me that she's plans for you which'll be very much to your advantage."

"Mrs. Cooper is being so sweet and understanding in saying that she will not stand in your way," Felicity said.

Carmela had only to look at her friend to know that her eyes were twinkling, and she was speaking in the soft, dulcet tones she used when she was manipulating someone to her own ends.

"It . . . it is very . . . kind of you," Carmela managed to stammer.

"I'll miss you—I don't pretend I shan't," Mrs. Cooper replied. "But Her Ladyship has promised to send me one of the young girls from the kitchen of the Castle to straighten things out, and that'll be a help, it will indeed!"

"I will send her as soon as I get back," Felicity said, "and thank you once again, dear Mrs. Cooper, for being so kind. Please remember me to the Vicar. As I will not be able to attend Church this Sunday because Carmela and I are going away, perhaps you will be kind enough to place my small offering in the plate?"

As Felicity spoke she opened a pretty satin reticule that she carried over her arm and took out a little mesh purse from which she counted out five golden guineas into Mrs. Cooper's outstretched hand.

"That is really very kind of you," Mrs. Cooper said in gratified tones. "Very, very kind!"

She transferred the coins into her other hand so that she could say good-bye to Carmela.

Then, with Felicity moving ahead like a ship in full sail and Carmela following almost as if she was mesmerised, they stepped into the carriage while Mrs. Cooper waved from the doorway as they drove off.

Only as the horses turned out through the narrow gate onto the roadway did Carmela say:

"Have you really . . . rescued me?"

"You certainly look as if you are in need of it," Felicity answered. "Dearest Carmela, how can all this have happened to you in such a short time?"

"Papa died at the end of January," Carmela replied,

"and I could not write to tell you, as I had no idea where you were."

"I was in France staying first with one of Grand-mama's friends, then another," Felicity replied, "so even if you had written to me, I doubt if the letter would have found me."

"You must miss her very, very much."

Felicity's grandmother with whom she had lived ever since she was a child had been the Dowager Countess of Galeston.

She had been a rather awe-inspiring lady and the people in the village had been very much in awe of her, but she had liked Carmela's mother and father and had even encouraged the latter in his painting by buying several of his pictures.

Because there were few children of Felicity's age in the neighbourhood whom her grandmother would allow her to know, Carmela was encouraged to visit the Castle, and when the two girls became inseparable it was obviously with the Countess's approval.

It was only as Felicity grew older that she went away often to stay with the Countess's friends, even though her grandmother was not well enough to accompany her.

This meant that Felicity's knowledge of the world was very different from Carmela's.

At the same time, as soon as she came home their friendship continued as before, and Carmela was content to be Felicity's confidante, listening to her adventures not with envy but with admiration.

"I was a success! A great success!" Felicity would boast after some interesting visit, and Carmela was only too ready to believe her.

It was just like old times, Carmela thought now, with Felicity telling her what to do and she being only too delighted and happy to oblige.

"What are your plans?" she asked as the carriage rolled on.

The horses turned through the imposing iron-work

gates with their attractive stone lodges on either side, which was the entrance to the mile-long drive to the Castle.

"That is what I am going to tell you," Felicity said, "and it is also why I need your help."

"My help?" Carmela asked.

Felicity turned towards her and said in a tone of voice very different from the one she had used before:

"You will help me, Carmela? Promise that you will help me!"

"Of course I will, dearest," Carmela replied. "You know I will do anything you want me to."

"That is what I knew you would say," Felicity said. "What I am going to ask may seem a little strange, but I knew when I came to find you that you would never fail me."

"Why should I?" Carmela asked in a puzzled tone. "You have always been so very, very sweet to me."

She waited, wondering why her friend was looking so serious, and she knew without words that she was going to ask her something unusual and perhaps difficult.

Felicity was looking ahead to where the Castle stood on a high piece of ground, its towers silhouetted against the sky.

It was built on an ancient site but it was in fact quite a modern Castle, which the Countess had bought from its previous owner when she was looking for somewhere to live after she had shaken the dust of Galeston from her feet.

Carmela had heard the story often enough.

The Countess had been a great beauty and a social personality of her time, and sometime after her son had inherited she had quarrelled with him and the rest of the family and finally decided that she would have nothing further to do with them.

Although she had always been a very dominating person and determined to have her own way in everything, they had not at first believed her.

But after a series of bitter and prolonged arguments,

and letters that sped back and forth between the Countess and the rest of the Gale family, she finally left the Dower House into which she had moved after her son had inherited.

Taking everything she possessed with her, the Countess told the Gales once and for all that she had no wish to see any of them again.

They found it hard to believe, especially as she had taken her son's young daughter with her.

This in fact had been one of the bones of contention between them, because Felicity's mother had died when she was born and the Countess had disapproved of the way in which she was being brought up.

Her son was more interested in his son and had allowed his mother to take charge of the upbringing of Felicity, thinking that the child might in fact sooner or later heal the breach between them.

The Countess, however, had moved to another part of England altogether and had no intention of being conciliatory.

As her son was nearly as obstinate as she was, the feud grew and grew until there ceased to be any communication between them.

Then the Countess had died, and when Felicity went to France to stay with some of her grandmother's friends, Carmela had wondered if she would turn towards the family she did not know.

This might be impossible, but it would obviously not be correct for her to live at the Castle alone without a Chaperone.

"We are going home," Felicity was saying, "and I will tell you the whole story as soon as we can be alone."

"You are making me very curious," Carmela said. "Is there anybody staying at the Castle?"

"No, not at the moment."

The way Felicity spoke sounded not quite natural, and Carmela could not help wondering what she had in store to tell her and how it concerned her personally.

At the same time, she was very thankful to leave the Vicarage.

She had always been deeply affected by her surroundings, and the ugliness of the Vicarage itself and the plainness of the children and their parents had been very hard to bear.

She had found it difficult to like either the Vicar or his wife, and although she knew she should be grateful to them, they were just not very pleasant people.

The Vicar particularly seemed to be lacking in Christian charity, and Mrs. Cooper was just a tiresome, neurotic woman who had too much to do and was not really fond of her children in spite of the fact that she had given them birth.

They were also comparative newcomers to the village, having lived there for only six years, while the previous Vicar had died after being the incumbent for over forty.

It was a joy for Carmela as she walked into the Castle to see again the perfect taste with which everything was arranged.

It was not only that the curtains were made of an expensive brocade, but they were exactly the right colour, just as the wall-coverings were restful and the pictures on them were a joy to look at.

There were also flowers arranged in large cut-glass vases that scented the atmosphere, and servants in smart uniforms smiling a welcome because they knew Carmela well and made her feel that, like Felicity, she had come home.

Felicity, handing her cloak to a footman and pulling off her bonnet, led the way into an attractive Sitting-Room that the two girls had always thought of as their own.

It had been furnished by the Countess with blue covers for the sofas and chairs which matched Felicity's eyes, and the pictures were in the Fragonard style, depicting ladies who Carmela thought had the same elegance as Felicity herself.

"Is there any refreshment you'd like, M'Lady?" the Butler asked from the door.

Felicity looked at Carmela, who shook her head.

"No, thank you, Bates."

The Butler closed the door and they were alone.

"You are sure you are not hungry?" Felicity asked. "You could not have eaten that filthy breakfast!"

"The very thought of it made me feel sick!" Carmela answered. "Oh, Felicity, I am hopeless at looking after children. At least—those children!"

"I am not surprised," Felicity answered. "But how could you do anything so stupid as to think that was where you would be happy?"

"What else could I do?" Carmela asked.

"You should have known I would have wanted you to come here," Felicity replied, "and do not pretend you were too proud, because I will not listen to you!"

They both laughed because it was an old joke about people being proud.

"When people talk about charity they always mean giving money," the Countess had said once. "But it is much more difficult and far more charitable to give one's self to people."

The two girls had thought this an amusing idea, and sometimes Felicity would go back to the Castle to say to her grandmother:

"I have been very charitable this afternoon, Grandmama. I talked for over ten mintues to that terrible old bore Miss Dobson, and I feel sure now I have moved up several places on the ladder to Heaven!"

"I am proud," Carmela said now, "but if you are thinking of being charitable to me, I am only too willing to accept."

"That is exactly what I want to do," Felicity said, "so now, dearest, listen to me."

"I am listening," Carmela answered, "and I have a strong feeling you are up to some mischief of some sort."

"I suppose that is what you might call it," Felicity agreed. "As it happens, I am going to be married!"

Carmela sat upright.

"Married? Oh, Felicity, how exciting! But . . . to whom?"

"To Jimmy—who else?"

Carmela was very still.

"Jimmy Salwick? But, Felicity, I did not know that his wife had died."

"She has not!"

Carmela looked at her friend wide-eyed.

"I . . . I do not . . . understand."

"She is dying, but she is not yet dead, and I am going away with Jimmy to France to stay there until we can be married."

There was silence. Then Carmela said:

"But, Felicity, you cannot do such a . . . thing! Think of your . . . reputation!"

"There are no arguments," Felicity said in a low voice. "This is something I must do, and, Carmela, you have to help me!"

Carmela looked worried.

She had known for over a year that Felicity was in love with Lord Salwick, who was a near neighbour.

He was an attractive, very charming young man who had inherited a large but dilapidated ancestral home and an impoverished Estate with no money to restore it.

Because Felicity had always known she would come into some money on her grandmother's death, they had been prepared to wait. She knew that if they approached the Countess she would make a great many difficulties because even if he were free she did not consider James Salwick, charming though he was, good enough for her granddaughter.

The Countess had always moved in the very highest of Society, and when she was young she had been a Lady of the Bed-Chamber to the Queen.

She had therefore set her heart on Felicity marrying one of the great noblemen who graced the Court, and she had compiled a list of the most eligible Dukes and Marquises whom she considered acceptable as her granddaughter's husband.

"It is no use arguing with Grandmama about Jimmy," Felicity had said often enough to Carmela. "You know how determined she is when she makes up her mind, and if I insist that I will marry no-one else, she will just make it impossible for us to see each other."

"I can understand that," Carmela replied, "but what will happen when she produces a man she considers an ideal husband for you?"

Fortunately that situation had not arisen, because the Countess became too ill and Felicity therefore was sent away to stay with her relatives, a number of whom, because the Countess had French blood in her, lived in France.

As soon as the war was over and France began to settle down again, Felicity was sent to stay in a huge *Château* on the Loire with aristocrats who in some miraculous manner had survived not only the Revolution but the social changes effected by Napoleon Bonaparte.

But the Countess's connections were not only French.

Felicity had travelled to Northumberland to stay with a Duke, to Cornwall to visit some of the ancient Cornish families who had eligible sons, and once she went even as far north as Edinburgh.

Although she always returned with stories of the people she had met and the men who had made love to her, when she was alone with Carmela she admitted that the only man who really meant anything to her was Jimmy Salwick.

When he was very young his parents had arranged his marriage to a wife who gradually became more and more mentally deranged until finally she was placed in a private Asylum.

It was a cruel fate for the young man because there was no way he could ever be rid of his wife except by her death, and he was tied to a woman he never saw.

It was inevitable that he should lose his heart to what was to all intents and purposes the girl next door.

It was not surprising that he loved Felicity, because, as Carmela saw when they were together, love made her glow with a radiance that any man with eyes in his head would have found irresistible.

At the same time, for Felicity to go away with him was to Carmela inconceivable.

"What I do not understand, dearest," she said now, "is why you cannot wait. If Jimmy's wife is dying, then surely as you have waited so long already, another few months or perhaps even a year would not matter?"

As she spoke she thought it would matter even less now that Felicity did not have her grandmother trying to force her to marry somebody else.

"I thought that was what you would say," Felicity replied, "but it is far more complicated than that."

"Why?"

"Because I have only just learnt when I returned to London from France that Grandmama has left me a huge fortune."

"A huge fortune?" Carmela repeated.

"It is enormous, really enormous!" Felicity said. "I never had the slightest idea that she had so much."

Carmela did not speak and after a moment Felicity went on:

"As you know, she quarrelled with Papa and all my other relatives. She said they were always battening on her, always expecting her to pay for everything, and it annoyed her."

"I always thought that living here she must be rich," Carmela said slowly.

"Yes, of course, rich by ordinary standards," Felicity agreed, "but not having a fortune that is so large that I cannot believe it! She kept it a secret."

"I suppose she did not wish your father to know about it."

"I realise that now," Felicity said, "but already it has begun to complicate things."

"Why?"

"Because as soon as the Solicitor came to see me," Felicity answered, "and he had been waiting for me to arrive back from France, I left London immediately and came here."

Carmela looked puzzled, and Felicity went on:

"I knew that I must go away with Jimmy before he heard of my fortune and before the Gales tried to get their hands on it."

Carmela looked bewildered.

"I . . . do not understand."

"It is quite simple," Felicity said. "First of all, if Jimmy knows how rich I am, he will not marry me."

"Why should you say that?" Carmela asked.

"Because he would be too proud," Felicity said, "and he will think that everybody will call him a fortune-hunter. In consequence he will leave me, and it will break my heart!"

The way Felicity spoke was very positive, and Carmela could not help agreeing that her reasoning was right.

James Salwick was a proud man. He disliked the fact that he could not repair his house or run his Estate the way he wished to do.

He was also in some ways almost ultra-sensitive about the tragedy of his wife, and Carmela was aware that he had at first fought against his feelings for Felicity because he had nothing to offer her.

It was Felicity who had fallen in love with him when they met out hunting and had made all the running.

Carmela knew how many excuses she had made to meet him when he was not expecting it, and that she had called at his house and had inveigled him under one pretext or another to come to the Castle.

When finally his feelings had been to much for him and he had confessed his love, Felicity had been frantic that she might lose him.

"He loves me, he loves me!" she had said to Carmela. "But he says he will never stand in my way, and if I want to marry somebody else, he will just disappear and I will never see him again!"

She gave a little cry of terror as she added:

"How can I lose him? Oh, Carmela, I cannot lose him!"

Thinking over what Felicity had said, Carmela understood now the danger if James Salwick knew how rich she was. Aloud she asked:

"Will he go away with you?"

"He will when he hears what next has happened."

"What is that?"

"I came back here from London the very moment I heard what the Solicitor had to tell me. And what do you think I found?"

"What?"

"A letter waiting here from Cousin Selwyn, the new Earl of Galeston."

"Why should he write to you?"

She knew that since Felicity's brother, who had been the pride, and joy of her father, had been killed just before Waterloo, the Earl when he died of a broken heart a year ago had no direct heir to follow him.

This meant that the title had gone to the son of his brother, who had married when he was very young.

Therefore, the present Earl of Galeston, Felicity's first cousin, was a considerably older man who had been a soldier without any prospects of inheriting the Earldom.

Carmela vaguely remembered hearing all this, but she had not been particularly interested because Felicity knew very little about her relatives, having never met them.

She had even learnt of her father's death only through the reports in the newspapers.

"Why should I care?" she had asked when Carmela pointed out the Obituary to her. "Grandmama hated him, and she told me often enough how much my father disliked me because I caused my mother's death when I was born."

"It seeems wrong somehow not to like your relations," Carmela had said.

"Nanny always said that you choose your friends, but your relatives are wished onto you," Felicity had retorted.

Then Carmela thought it was obvious, since Felicity was now alone in the world, that her relatives would be interested in her, although it seemed rather late after there had been no communication from them since she was five.

"What did the new Earl have to say to you?" she asked.

Felicity's lips tightened and in a hard voice she said:

"He informed me that as Grandmama was dead he was now my Guardian, and he ordered me, as if I were one of his Troops, to come to Galeston immediately as he had plans for my future."

Carmela gasped.

"I cannot believe he wrote like that!"

"He did! You shall see the letter, and if he thinks I am going to obey him, he is very much mistaken."

"But . . . if he is your Guardian . . . ?"

"He is asserting himself as my Guardian now only because he has heard about the money Grandmama left me," Felicity interrupted. "I am not a fool. If it had been just a small amount on which I could live without any fuss, Cousin Selwyn would not have bothered about me or been interested as to whether I lived or died. But now that I am an heiress, it is a very different thing!"

"How can you be sure he is like that?" Carmela asked.

She hated the hard note in Felicity's voice and the hard expression that was in her eyes.

It somehow spoilt her beauty, and Carmela loved her too much to wish her ever to be bitter or cynical.

"Grandmama said they were a 'money-grubbing' lot, and she was right!" Felicity said. "I am quite certain that now that he has heard of the millions I own, Cousin Selwyn wants to get his grubby hands on it!"

"Oh, Felicity, that is going too far!" Carmela protested.

"Why are you sticking up for him?" Felicity asked. "Papa died a full ten months ago, but only now, after Grandmama's death, is the new Earl *ordering* me to come to Galeston. I would rather die!"

"You do not mean that!"

Felicity suddenly laughed.

"No, I do not mean it. I am going to live and marry Jimmy quickly, before he learns how rich I am. Once we are marrried, there will be nothing that either he or the Earl can do about it!"

"That is true enough," Carmela agreed. "But you cannot marry Jimmy until . . . his wife is . . . dead."

"She is dying! I told you that! Jimmy had a letter from the Surgeon who is looking after her, saying that she has a brain-tumour. I have asked a number of people about it, and a person with a brain-tumour never lives very long."

"I cannot pretend I am sorry," Carmela said, "but at the same time, please wait, Felicity. Please wait before you do anything . . . foolish."

"I am not taking any risks on that score!"

"But supposing the Earl finds you wherever you hide and brings you back?"

"That is the threat which I am going to use to Jimmy to make him take me away," Felicity said. "I

shall show him Cousin Selwyn's letter, and he will
know he means business."

She paused before she continued:

"He will guess there is an ulterior motive in his
interest, but I shall not let him think it is money, but
only that I am a Gale and therefore come under his
jurisdiction because I am young, and of course—
attractive!"

"Do you think Jimmy will believe you?"

"He will believe it because he will want to, and
you know as well as I do, Carmela, that he really loves
me."

Felicity's voice softened and Carmela said quickly:

"Yes, darling, I know he does, and you love him.
At the same time, it is . . . wrong for you to be . . . together unless you are . . . man and wife."

As she spoke Carmela thought it was very shocking
indeed, but she did not want to upset Felicity by saying
so.

However, Felicity saw the expression on her face
and gave a little laugh.

"I can see what you are thinking, Carmela. At the
same time, I do not think you need worry about me.
Jimmy himself is so protective that I am quite certain
he will not do anything you think wrong until I am
really his wife."

Her chin quivered as she went on:

"At the same time, if there is a question of Cousin
Selwyn trying to annul the marriage because I am
under-age, I shall make quite certain that I am having a
baby!"

Carmela gave a cry of protest, but Felicity put out
her hand to take hers.

"Please, dearest, I know what I am doing. Jimmy
is everything that matters to me, and my whole happiness rests on our being together. That is why you have
to help me."

"I . . . cannot see what I . . . can do," Carmela said.

"It is quite simple," Felicity answered. "You will go to Galeston in my place and stay there until I am married to Jimmy!"

Chapter Two

"I cannot do it . . . it is impossible!" Carmela said over and over again.

But she knew her voice was beginning to weaken as she felt she would not be able to resist Felicity much longer.

It had always been the same ever since they were children.

When Felicity made up her mind to do something, she was so determined and so plausible that it was impossible to say "no."

"Of course they will know I am not you," Carmela protested.

"Why should they?" Felicity asked. "None of my relatives have seen me since I was five, and until now, as you well know, they have not been interested in me."

She paused before she said bitterly:

"There was not a single letter from any of my cousins, my great-aunts, or my other relatives asking me to live with them after Grandmama died, until this one from Cousin Selwyn!"

She went on in a contemptuous tone:

"He is quite obviously interested only in my fortune. In fact, my Solicitor told me that he was the only person who knew about it!"

"How was your grandmother able to keep such a momentous secret from everybody?" Carmela asked.

27

"Apparently a great deal of her money is invested in Jamaica and has multiplied enormously in the last few years because of the demand for sugar. The Solicitor told me that her investments in England also have been very productive. They must have been, seeing the amount she has left me."

Carmela did not speak and after a moment Felicity sighed.

"This is a great responsibility and not really a blessing. I know that Jimmy will dislike my being so rich, and I shall never know whether people like me for myself or for what I possess."

"People will always love you because you are you," Carmela said impulsively, and Felicity smiled.

"That is what I want to hear," she said, "and I do not wish to become like Grandmama, who hated all the Gales because she felt they were after her money."

"Please do not let it spoil you," Carmela pleaded, "and I do understand how worrying it is to have so much and to have to hide it from Jimmy."

"If you understand that, you will help me," Felicity said quickly.

"But no-one will believe I am you," Carmela protested again.

"Why not?" Felicity enquired. "You are just as pretty as I am, and when you are dressed in my clothes we will not look unalike, in fact we might even be sisters."

There was some truth in this, for both girls were fair, both had blue eyes, and both had perfect pink-and-white complexions which were the admiration of the men and the envy of the women.

But while Felicity had a sophisticated elegance, Carmela looked like a simple country girl and lacked the polish which clothes and self-assurrance could give.

Felicity looked at Carmela now with a critical eye, then rose to her feet and took her by the hand.

"Come with me," she said, "we are going upstairs."

"What for?" Carmela asked.

"You are going to be made to look exactly like me," Felicity replied. "We will start by arranging your hair in a fashionable style, and I have already decided that you shall have all the gowns I have been wearing since Grandmama died."

Carmela thought that would be very appropriate because she was aware that Felicity was wearing mauve as half-mourning.

She herself had not been able to afford any new gowns after her father's death, in fact all she could do was to change the ribbons on her bonnet and wear a black sash.

As she walked beside Felicity she was acutely conscious of how threadbare was the gown she was wearing.

Also, as she had not changed before she left the Vicarage, there were not only some dirty marks on her skirt but there were also a few spots of egg which Lucy had splattered over her.

They went up the broad staircase to the beautiful bedroom where Felicity had always slept.

There were several trunks on the floor, but they were not yet unpacked and there was no maid in the room.

"As I am going away tomorrow," Felicity explained before Carmela could question her, "I told them to unpack nothing. But these are the trunks you will be taking with you, and they contain all my latest clothes, which are either black or mauve."

"What are you going to wear?" Carmela asked with a little smile.

"I am going to make Jimmy take me to Paris and fit me out with an entire new wardrobe."

"Paris? Is that wise?"

"As it happens, Grandmama's French friends all live in other parts of France, so I am not likely to meet them. If I do, I shall just introduce Jimmy as my husband, and there is no reason why they should question it."

"You seem very sure that Jimmy will agree to this fantastic plan of yours."

As Carmela spoke she saw the expression of anxiety in Felicity's eyes before she replied:

"If Jimmy loves me as I know he does, he will not want me to go to Galeston to be pressurised into marriage with somebody chosen for me by Cousin Selwyn."

"Do you really think that is what he intends?"

"I am sure of it!" Felicity said. "And I do not mind betting that it is a relation of some sort, so that they can keep the money in the family."

Carmela did not argue, as she felt there was nothing she could say.

At the same time, she could not believe that the Gales were quite as unpleasant as Felicity made them out to be.

Yet, she was well aware that a Guardian, like a parent, had complete control over a young girl until she was twenty-one.

If the present Earl wished Felicity to marry, then he could arrange it and there was nothing whatever she could do to prevent herself being taken up the aisle and married off to some man she did not love.

Because her own parents had been so happy, Carmela had always assumed that she and Felicity would someday be happy in the same way, and there was no doubt that Jimmy was the only man for Felicity.

"I still think what you are doing is . . . wrong," she said in a low voice, but even as she spoke she was aware that Felicity was not listening to her.

She had thrown open the lid of the trunk which had already been unstrapped and unlocked.

"I remember noticing what the maids in London put on top of this trunk," she said, "and just now I thought it is exactly what you need to travel in."

"I see you were not expecting me to refuse you," Carmela observed.

"How could you when it matters so much to me?"

Felicity asked. "If it were the other way round, you know I would save you."

"As you have already done," Carmela said with a smile.

"From those ghastly children, and however ferocious Cousin Selwyn may be, he could not be worse than Henry Cooper!"

Carmela laughed. Then she said in a serious tone:

"I feel very . . . frightened at the thought of . . . going to Galeston expecting at any . . . moment to be . . . exposed."

"It cannot be for long," Felicity said soothingly. "The moment I am married to Jimmy, you will be able to leave."

"What am I to do then?"

"You are to go to Jimmy's house here and wait until we return from abroad. Then we will discuss your future, and I promise you, dearest, it will be a very happy, comfortable one."

"You know I cannot accept money from you . . ." Carmela began in an uncomfortable tone.

"If you talk like that, I shall slap you!" Felicity said. "If you think I am going to listen to both you and Jimmy talking about my money as though it is contaminated, I shall put everything I possess in a bag and throw it into the sea!"

The way she spoke made Carmela laugh, but she said:

"I shall find something to do which will earn me enough to live on."

"What you will have to do is to get married," Felicity said. "We will find you a charming husband very nearly as nice as Jimmy, and you will live happily ever afterwards."

"I think that is unlikely . . ." Carmela began, but Felicity was pulling the gowns out of the trunk and the words died on her lips.

Never had she imagined that gowns in various shades of mauve could be so lovely and so alluring.

There was also a white gown embroidered with violets, with ribbons to match, and an evening-gown that glittered with embroidery which looked like amethysts and diamonds.

"Were you really . . . expecting to wear . . . those?" Carmela asked.

"Of course!" Felicity replied. "And to tell you the truth, dearest, I am sick to death of them! I miss Grandmama, I miss her terribly, but you know she always said that people who mourned someone for too long were bores, and if one were a Christian one believed anyway that they were not dead but alive in Heaven."

"Mama used to think the same thing," Carmela replied, "and anyway, I could not afford to buy any mourning for Papa."

"Then you can wear these clothes for another month or two, and if Jimmy's wife is not dead by then I will send you some coloured gowns from Paris."

"Will that not seem strange?" Carmela asked.

"With the money you are supposed to own, you can be dressed from head to foot in gold and diamonds!"

"That is what I shall feel like in these dresses," Carmela answered.

"Then hurry and put them on," Felicity said. "And I must do somethng about your hair."

An hour later, Carmela was staring at herself in the mirror in a bemused fashion.

She was wearing a pale gown the colour of Parma violets, and these was a large bunch of those flowers at her waist.

Felicity's lady's-maid Martha had arranged her hair in an exact copy of her mistress's, and when she had added a little powder to Carmela's small straight nose and a touch of salve to her lips, they might almost have been twins.

Martha, who had been with Felicity for years and

knew Carmela well, was the only person to be let into the secret of what the two girls were about to do.

"It's not that I approves of what Her Ladyship's up to," Martha had said to Carmela, "but once she's set her heart on something, it's no use arguing with her."

"That is true," Carmela had said, "but do you think, Martha, that anybody will believe for one moment that I am really Her Ladyship?"

"You wait until I've finished with you, Miss," Martha had replied, and Carmela had to admit now that she looked very unlike herself.

"Be very careful what you say downstairs, Martha," Felicity warned, "except that we are all leaving tomorrow."

"They knows that already," Martha said, "but they didn't ask me any questions."

"That is a blessing."

Martha went from the room to fetch something, and Carmela asked:

"How can you be sure of anything until Jimmy agrees?"

"He will agree," Felicity said confidently, "and he should be arriving anytime now."

"Will you want to see him alone?" Carmela asked.

"Yes, of course," Felicity answered. "I am going to show him Cousin Selwyn's letter. I know then he will agree to all my plans."

Carmela hesitated for a moment. Then she said:

"Do you not think, Felicity dearest, that it would be more honest if you told him the truth? When after you have married him he finds out that you have been deceitful about your money, will it not make him angry and feel that he cannot trust you in the future?"

She knew by the way Felicity's lips tightened that she had thought about this already and knew the answer.

"That is a risk I have to take," she said, "but I cannot help feeling that when Jimmy is married to me, nothing will be of any importance except the fact that we are together."

That, Carmela was to think later, was the truth.

She had only to see Lord Salwick looking at Felicity to know that he loved her with all his heart and that his idea of perfect happiness was for her to be his wife.

He arrived just before luncheon, and Felicity had no time to tell him what was happening. So they ate first, a small but delicious meal cooked by a Chef who had been at the castle for ten years with the Countess.

Because Lord Salwick was obviously so pleased to see Felicity again, he could not take his eyes off her, and while they tried to talk sensibly of what they had each been doing while they were apart, there were moments when their words died away and they could only look at each other with love in their eyes.

Carmela had been amused when she first went down to the Drawing-Room before luncheon to find that for a moment Lord Salwick did not recognise her.

Then he had exclaimed:

"You have changed, Carmela! I thought you were one of Felicity's smart friends she had brought here from London."

"No, I am just myself," Carmela answered, "but 'fine feathers make fine birds'!"

"Oh, you have some new clothes," Lord Salwick said vaguely, "and you are doing your hair in a new way."

"It is like mine," Felicity said, "and I will tell you all about it, darling, after luncheon."

As soon as Felicity spoke, Carmela realised that Lord Salwick had forgotten her and had turned his attention to Felicity as if she filled his whole world.

As soon as the meal was over Carmela went upstairs.

"I will send for you when I have made Jimmy agree to everything," Felicity had said before he arrived.

"Be careful not to tell too many lies!"

"Yes of course," Felicity agreed.

Once Carmela was alone upstairs in Felicity's bedroom, she looked at the trunk which she knew contained more clothes than she had ever worn in her whole life, and the doubts as to whether she was doing the right thing, or something that was utterly and completely mad, came crowding back into her mind.

Then she told herself that the only thing that really mattered was that she should help Felicity because she loved her and should not think of herself.

At the same time, to go to a strange house and live with strange people, especially the Gales, who sounded terrifying, was almost as bad as returning to the Vicarage and being confronted by the obstreperous children again.

"I must be brave and adventurous," Carmela told herself, although she felt neither of those things, but just helpless, as she had felt when her father died.

Supposing she let Felicity down? Supposing the moment she arrived one of the family whom Felicity had forgotten about denounced her as an imposter?

There were dozens of disasters that might happen, and because she had lived such a quiet, uneventful life she thought she would never be able to carry off an impersonation of Felicity, who was used to parties, dinners, Balls, and Receptions, and had often travelled abroad.

"Perhaps the Gales will not know that," Carmela tried to console herself, but she had the uncomfortable feeling that there would always be prying eyes and gossipping tongues!

Some kind friend would be only too willing to tittle-tattle about the Countess who had cut herself off from the rest of the family and brought up a very beautiful granddaughter without their help.

Because she felt perturbed and anxious, Carmela walked to the window and as she did so caught a glimpse of herself in the long mirror.

For a moment she could hardly believe she was seeing her own reflection. Then she told herself that

whatever her inner fears might be, outwardly she really
did look the part she was to play.

She would not have been human if she had not felt
it a joy to wear a gown that was more beautiful and
more elegant than anything she had ever worn before.

'I am sure if Papa could see me he would want to
paint me,' she thought.

Then she knew that her father would be more
likely to paint her as a nymph wearing something
diaphanous that looked like the mist on the water or
perhaps a sky sprinkled with stars if he was painting her
at night.

'For the moment I am content with these real
gowns,' Carmela thought with a smile.

She looked at those which Felicity had flung on the
bed, thinking she had never imagined she would ever be
able to wear anything that looked as if it had stepped
straight out of a dream.

When there was a knock on the door and one of
the servants asked her to go downstairs, she felt as if the
sound jerked her back to reality.

She swallowed apprehensively as she entered the
Drawing-Room, where Felicity and Lord Salwick were
waiting.

They were both looking very happy, and Felicity,
who was holding his hand, did not relinquish it as he
rose to his feet.

"Come and talk to us, dearest Carmela," she said. "I
have told Jimmy how kind you have promised to be and
he is very grateful."

"I am indeed, Carmela!" Lord Salwick said. "But it
seems we are asking a great deal of you."

"I . . . I want to . . . help," Carmela said quietly.

"And you will help us by staying at Galeston just
until we are married," Felicity said.

"I only hope that I can . . . act the part skilfully."

"I can see now that you do look rather like Felicity," Lord Salwick said, "only . . ."

He stopped as if he realised that what he meant

would sound rude, and Carmela finished the sentence for him.

". . . Only she is much, much lovelier than I could ever be."

"That is what I thought," Lord Salwick smiled, "but of course I am prejudiced."

"That is what I hope you will always be," Felicity said. "Otherwise, I warn you, Jimmy, I shall be very, very jealous!"

"Not half as jealous as I shall be about you," he said. "If you even look at another man I will murder him!"

Felicity laughed in delight, and taking his hand held it against her cheek.

"We are going to be very happy," she said, "and there will be no time for anybody else in our lives except ourselves."

"You can be sure of that, my darling," Lord Salwick said. "But I wish it were easier and we could be married right away."

"I am sure it will not be long," Felicity said confidently, "and I cannot risk losing you."

"You will never do that," he said, "and although I think it is something I should not do, I cannot risk your obeying your cousin's summons and finding that he intends to marry you off to somebody else."

"I am sure that is what he intends," Felicity replied. "Otherwise, why should he have sent for me so suddenly when there have been no previous communications?"

"I agree, it is all very suspicious," Lord Salwick said, "and therefore we will do what you wish. I must go home now and make arrangements for the house and the horses to be looked after while I am away."

"Yes, of course!" Felicity said. "And you will not forget that I want one of your men to drive Carmela to London?"

Carmela looked surprised and Felicity explained:

"It would be a great mistake for old Gibbons to take you. We could not be sure he would not gossip with the servants at Galeston House, and another thing—he would forget to call you 'M'Lady.'"

"I can understand that," Carmela said, "but..."

"It is all arranged," Felicity interrupted. "Jimmy has a new coachman who has never seen you, and he is going to tell him to come here and drive a lady he will think is me to London in Grandmama's carriage, which, as you know, had the coat-of-arms on the door."

"And when I...get to...Galeston House in... London?" Carmela asked in a low voice.

"Cousin Selwyn had made arrangements for me to stay the night there and his horses will take you to Galeston the next day. He had it all 'cut and dried,' obviously not expecting me to be able to think for myself."

"Perhaps he is just being polite and considerate," Lord Salwick suggested quietly.

"To suit his own ends!" Felicity replied. "Do not forget, darling Jimmy, he never wrote to me when Grandmama died."

"I agree that was inexcusable."

"Now I am just wondering," Felicity said, "which of the impoverished, spendthrift Gales he is expecting me to marry."

Carmela looked at her warningly, fearing that Lord Salwick might suspect how rich she really was.

Then she remembered that even without the very large fortune she now had inherited, it would have been expected that Felicity should have some money left to her by her grandmother as well as the Castle and its contents.

As if Felicity realised what she was thinking, she said:

"I am keeping the Castle open for the time being until Jimmy can arrange everything for me and decide what we will move from here into his own house."

"Then would it not be better, when I know you are...married, for me to...come...here?" Carmela asked.

Felicity shook her head.

"You may have to run away, and if Cousin Selwyn tries to pursue you or wishes to make himself unpleasant, it would be better for you to be somewhere where he would not find you."

"Y-yes . . . of course," Carmela said hesitatingly, "but I hope he will not be very . . . very . . . angry when he knows he has been . . . deceived."

Felicity shrugged her shoulders.

"What does it matter if he is? I will be married by then, and we will look after you, will we not, darling Jimmy?"

"Of course," Lord Salwick agreed. "We will see that you do not have to go back to work at the Vicarage or anywhere else for that matter, and I am very sorry about your father. I did not know until Felicity told me that he had died."

Carmela felt the tears come into hr eyes and for the moment she could not answer.

Felicity put her arms round her.

"It is all right, dearest," she said. "You are not alone any longer. You are with us! We love you and you will never again have to suffer as you have had to do by working for people like the Coopers."

"They . . . meant to be . . . kind," Carmela said with a little choke in her voice.

"No-one could be kind who possessed a son like that monster Henry!" Felicity answered.

Because it somehow sounded ridiculous, Carmela gave a choked little laugh.

"I really ought to go," Lord Salwick said. "Will you be ready if I fetch you in my travelling-carriage at nine o'clock?"

"Of course I will!" Felicity replied. "I shall have very little luggage because I am going to buy a whole trousseau in France in which you will think I look beautiful."

"How could you be anything else?" he said.

"Nobody knows anything except for Carmela and

Martha," Felicity said. "I shall just tell the servants that
I am going back to London."

"Are you going to stay there the night?" Carmela
asked, knowing she also would be in London at Galeston
House.

"Yes, but not in Grandmama's house, in case somebody should hear of it," Felicity replied. "I shall stay at
an Hotel under an assumed name, and only when we
get to France will Jimmy and I be known as Lord and
Lady Salwick."

"Which you will be very, very soon," Lord Salwick
said in a low voice.

"That is all I want, now and forever," Felicity
replied.

They looked into each other's eyes and Carmela
was forgotten.

Then, because she knew they wanted to say good-
bye to each other, she slipped from the room and left
them alone.

Because she had got her own way and everything
appeared to be "plain sailing," Felicity was in sparkling
spirits all the evening.

They laughed as she and Carmela reminisced about
when they were children, and only when they went up
to bed early did Felicity say in a more serious
tone:

"I am very, very grateful to you, dearest! I cannot
live without Jimmy, and this is the only way I can be
sure of not losing him."

"I do not think you would ever do that," Carmela
answered.

"I am giving you some money," Felicity went on.
"I know how humiliating it must have been at the
Vicarage to be without it."

They went into her bedroom and she took a sealed
package from one of the drawers of the dressing-table,
saying:

"There is one hundred pounds here, some in notes,
some in sovereigns."

"One hundred pounds?" Carmela exclaimed. "I do not need as much as that!"

"Of course you do," Felicity said firmly, "and there is also a cheque for another hundred pounds, which you can cash anytime you want, from Coutts Bank in London."

"It is too much," Carmela protested.

"Remember, you are supposed to be well off, if not a millionairess," Felicity admonished. "You must tip generously and keep enough money with which to run away whe the time comes. You may have to come back in a post-chaise. Anyway, it is fatal not to be able to pay one's way, and I am making sure you can do that."

"You are so . . . kind," Carmela said softly.

"Not in the least! You are being kind to me," Felicity answered, "and I have every intention of giving you all the money you need in the future, so there is no need to pinch and starve."

Carmela was about to say that her pride would not let her take it. Then the old joke about "pride and charity" occurred to them both and they laughed.

"Do not dare say it!" Felicity admonished. "You are my responsibility from now on, and let me say that because I am being married first, I already feel as if you are my debutante daughter and I have to launch you on the Social World."

They both laughed again because it sounded absurd, but when she was alone Carmela could not help feeling that it was almost true.

Because Felicity was so much more worldly-wise and sophisticated compared to herself, Carmela felt she was like an unfledged School-girl stepping into a world of which she knew nothing and would therefore appear gauche and unsure of herself.

At the same time, she could feel a sense of adventure seeping through her because it was so exciting to have such beautiful clothes and to get away from the Vicarage.

"God will look after me," she told herself before she fell asleep.

She felt quite sure too that her father and mother were near her and they would somehow protect her from any extreme consequences of the deception on which she was embarking to help Felicity.

"Whatever happens," Carmela said, "I will try not to have any regrets."

* * *

The Earl of Galeston was sitting in the Library at Galeston Park with a map of the Estate spread out in front of him.

"As I have not been here since I was a small boy," he said to the Manager standing beside him, "you must remind me of the names of the woods and the farms, and of course I shall want to know about the present tenants."

"I think Your Lordship will find I have set it all down in the memorandum I laid before you when you arrived."

"I have read it," the Earl replied, "but I did not find it as comprehensive as I would wish."

He knew as he spoke that the man beside him was anxious, and he thought that his suspicions were fully justified. It was quite obvious that the Manager was not only incompetent and lazy but very probably dishonest also.

The Earl had come to Galeston with an open mind, knowing that it would be a great mistake to make changes too quickly. In the words in which he would have advised a young Subaltern just joining the Regiment, he must "play himself in."

The Earl had never in his wildest dreams expected to inherit the title or any of the Estates.

As his father was a younger son he had always known that in the usual English tradition, the family money all belonged to the reigning Earl, while his brother and certainly his nephew could expect nothing.

He had therefore chosen the Army as his career

and expected to stay in the Regiment until he retired.

Because he was a good soldier, he rose through sheer merit rather than by buying promotions, and he was actually a Colonel before, like being hit by a bombshell, he learnt that his uncle had died unexpectedly and he was the seventh Earl of Galeston.

Of course he had known that the direct heir, his cousin, had been killed just before his twenty-first birthday.

But as his uncle was a comparatively young man who had been a widower for a long time, and if he thought about it at all, Selwyn Gale had assumed that the Earl would marry again and do his best to produce another son.

The thought indeed had just passed through his mind, then he forgot it, being too busy soldiering to have any other interests.

He had spent some years in India when he first joined the Regiment, then had come back with Sir Arthur Wellesley to join him in his campaigns against Napoleon in Portugal and Spain, and finally he had gone to France to defeat the French Emperor at the Battle of Waterloo.

Selwyn Gale had then been busy in the Army of Occupation, and it was only several months after succeeding to the title that he very reluctantly said good-bye to the Army and started a life that was very different from anything he had ever known before.

To begin with, he was overwhelmed by the amount of his possessions and the importance and authority that went with his new position.

He was also astonished to discover how rich he was.

Lack of money had always been a handicap in his life, and he now found it almost as difficult to accustom himself to being a rich man as to cope with the problems of being poor.

At the same time, he could not help thinking that the years of comparative poverty had taught him lessons that he would never forget, besides having given him an understanding and sympathy for those who had to pinch and save as he had been obliged to do.

However, there was one thing which infuriated him, and that was any form of dishonesty.

He had been quick to detect among those whom he commanded any who stole, cheated, or were deceitful in obtaining money they could not earn honestly.

When he inherited he was shrewdly aware that a rich man was considered "fair game" by those who knew how to profit from any blindness or carelessness on his part.

He therefore took things slowly, noting unnecessary extravagances here and there, but saying nothing.

He watched for any who were filling their own pockets at his expense and was waiting to strike at those who were definitely "fiddling the books" until they should have no defence against his accusations.

He looked at the map in front of him again before he said:

"I see you have sold a great deal of timber recently, Matthews. I would like an account of what the wood fetched and who bought it."

The Manager's eyes flickered, and the Earl was aware that this was another discrepancy in the accounts that had been handed to him.

"What is more," he said, "I have been unable to locate a number of farm implements which are listed here, but which have, I assume, been placed in some part of the Estate where I can inspect them!"

Now the Manager was tense, and the Earl knew without being told that the accounts had been falsified, and half the items that had been entered as having been bought had no substance in fact.

"Let me have all this information by tomorrow morning, Matthews," he said, "and when you bring it I would also like to see the Estate Accountant at the same time."

"That'll be Lane, M'Lord."

"I am aware of that," the Earl said, "and as I would not wish to waste more time than necessary, tell him to bring his books here within the hour so that I shall have a chance to peruse them."

The Manager's face now had an unhealthy pallor, and the Earl knew he had been right in suspecting that he and the Accountant had been working together and the books were well and truly "cooked."

He rose to his feet.

"That will be all, Matthews," he said. "I will see you at ten o'clock tomorrow morning."

"Very good, M'Lord."

The Manager walked towards the door.

He had almost reached it when he stopped, and the Earl knew he was trying to make up his mind whether to make a clean breast of what he had done or to hand in his resignation.

Finally he decided to do neither but walked from the room, and his footsteps going down the passage seemed to get slower and slower as he went.

The Earl was certain that by tomorrow morning he would either have packed up and left or would try to make the Accountant the scapegoat, forcing him to take the blame for what had occurred.

His lips were set in a hard line as he thought how gullible his uncle had been in trusting such a man.

What was more, he suspected that he was just one of many who would eventually have to leave the Estate to be replaced by men who were more honest.

It was depressing, to say the least of it, to find that things were not as he had hoped and that he was not being served by trustworthy servants who thought of their positions as a privilege and revered the family to which they owed their allegiance.

Then the Earl thought that he was being absurdly idealistic to expect so much.

There were crooks in every walk of life, and even amidst the beauty and grandeur of Galeston he must expect them to show their heads like reptiles.

He had hoped—of course it was but a faint hope—that because his inheritance was so fine and he was so intensely proud of it, everything would be perfect.

But he was just a fool to think that anything in life could be like that! Instead, he would have to work and fight to attain the perfection he sought and must expect to be disillusioned a dozen times in the process.

All the same, as he stood at a window which looked out over the lake to the great trees in the Park and thought of the ten thousand acres that surrounded him, a feeling of satisfaction seemed to well up in him almost like a paean of joy.

It was his—his for his lifetime and, if he was fortunate, for the sons who would follow him.

'I will not be such a fool as to have only one son,' the Earl thought to himself, remembering how his cousin had been killed in action. 'I want a dozen!'

Then he laughed because he knew he first had to find a wife.

That might not be so difficult now that he was in a position to be able to offer so much to the woman he married.

When he was a soldier he had thought it would be impossible for him ever to be able to afford to marry, unless he chose a rich wife. And that was unlikely not only because he disliked women who had more money than himself, but also because the women who attracted him would find it impossible to live on a soldier's pay.

In the course of his service in different lands there had been a number of lovely ladies with whom Selwyn Gale, being a very handsome and attractive man, had had fiery liaisons.

However, they had lasted only the short time he could spare between his varying duties.

But just as he had known that none of them was likely to become a permanent feature of his life, so the ladies in question, although they loved the strength of his arms, the fire of his kisses, and the sensations he aroused in them, had no intention of being "camp followers."

"I love you, Selwyn!" one of the most beautiful of his *affaires de coeur* had said to him one night. "Why, dearest, could you not be a rich Duke or a wealthy Marquis, so that if Harry died, which is very likely from the way he is drinking at the moment, we could live happily ever after?"

Although it was a sentimental moment, Selwyn Gale had not been able to prevent himself from thinking a little cynically that the love which she had just demonstrated very effectively was not the sort that lasted.

In fact, he had been quite certain that by the time he returned to his Regiment, the lady now in his arms would be consoling herself very effectively with one of his brother-Officers.

What was more, he had known, if he was honest, that although he found her very alluring, he would seldom think of her once they had parted.

Marriage was something which had never entered into his plans, except perhaps for when he was about to retire and would want somebody to keep him company in the long winter evenings.

Now at thirty-three the future was very different, and he knew that marriage to somebody suitable who would be the mother of his children was certainly an important item on his programme.

"I shall have to think about it when I have got the Estate straight," he decided.

He admitted he had never been happier in his whole life than in reorganising and rearranging not only his house and Estates but also himself.

That was what he had always enjoyed doing, and although in the Regiment they used to laugh at him for wanting to change things and improve them, he had a taste for organisation that he could never lose.

Just as he planned his tactics in battle so that he

invariably lost fewer men than any other Commander, so now he planned his improvements on the Estate and was ready to plan his own life down to the last detail.

"First things first!" he told himself as he looked out on the Park.

The door opened behind him and he heard his Butler say:

"His Royal Highness Prince Frederich has arrived, M'Lord! I have shown him into the Blue Salon."

"Thank you, Newman, I will join him there," the Earl replied.

He turned back for a moment to take another look at the sunshine outside.

Here was another problem to solve, but he thought with satisfaction that he had the answer to that.

Everything was under control, and the knowledge gave him a feeling of immense satisfaction.

Then, as if it was an effort, he turned away from the view and walked towards the door of the Library.

As he did so he forced himself to put his own problems to one side while he contemplated those of the Prince who was waiting for him in the Blue Salon.

He remembered that Napoleon had spoken of the "cupboards of the mind," and he thought it a good expression for the practice of keeping things in their own compartments, so that one closed one cupboard-door before opening another one.

The idea amused him, and there was a smile on his lips as he walked quickly down the long corridor furnished with treasures collected over the centuries by members of the Gale family to the Blue Salon, where Prince Frederich was waiting.

Chapter Three

As the Earl's carriage, drawn by four extremely fine horses, drew nearer to Galeston Park, Carmela felt more and more frightened.

It had been exciting to drive to London yesterday in the Countess's carriage, which she knew so well, and even when she arrived at Galeston House in Park Lane she did not feel overwhelmingly nervous.

This was because she was quite certain, from the letter which Felicity had shown her, that the Earl would not be there.

Instead there was his Secretary, an elderly man with delightful manners, who welcomed Carmela as if she were an old friend and spoke respectfully of the Countess, whom he had known in the past.

Because she was tired after the long journey, she was glad to have supper on a tray in her bedroom and then get into bed.

On Felicity's instructions, she had explained fulsomely but convincingly that the reason she had to travel alone was that her lady's-maid had unfortunately been taken ill at the last moment, and she had been obliged to leave her behind.

"I considered delaying my arrival," she said to the Earl's Secretary, "but I thought that might be inconvenient to His Lordship, and therefore I came alone."

"It is extremely unfortunate for you, M'Lady," the

Secretary replied, "but I will make sure you are accompanied on the journey to Galeston tomorrow by one of our senior staff."

After a comparatively restful night Carmela was slightly amused to meet the elderly housemaid who was to chaperone her on the drive to the country.

With a beaded bonnet on her grey hair and a severe black cape over her plain dress, she looked a picture of propriety, and Carmela thought that nobody at Galeston could be anything but impressed by her arrival.

They talked on the journey, and Carmela learnt a lot that she wanted to know.

First, that the Earl had only in the last two months returned from the Continent.

That of course, she realised, explained why he had not known of the Countess's death and had not attended her Funeral or even sent a wreath.

He was also, she was informed by the housemaid, "a fine upstanding gentleman" but was used to commanding soldiers.

This information made Carmela certain that Felicity was right in saying that he was very autocratic and would not expect anyone to go against his wishes.

The housemaid went on talking about the old days, and Carmela sensed that the staff were nervous of the recent innovations, new ideas, and new duties that they had not had to undertake in the past.

All this seemed rather disturbing, and Carmela began to dislike the idea of meeting the Earl and being for even a short time under his jurisdiction.

If she had been doubtful whether Felicity had been wise in running away with Lord Salwick before they were married, she could not help feeling now that her friend might have risked her whole happiness if she had gone to Galeston as she had been ordered to do.

'I must be very careful not to be unmasked until Felicity and Jimmy are married,' Carmela thought.

She sent up a little prayer that Jimmy's mad wife

would die soon and that Felicity, whom she loved, would be really happy with him.

The only thing that gave her any confidence was her new clothes.

The housemaids had been horrified that she should wear the same gown today as she had worn yesterday.

They had therefore unpacked a very attractive one of white muslin with a hem embroidered with mauve pansies and ribbons which matched her high-crowned bonnet.

Over it was a tight-fitting and very elegant coat of pale mauve silk with purple buttons and a velvet collar and cuffs in the same hue.

She thought it looked so fashionable that it might have come from Paris, and the maids thought the same.

"I wish you was stayin' here, M'Lady," they said, "so that we could see all your pretty clothes. It's a long time since we had any really smart ladies in the house."

"I expect the Earl will soon be giving parties," Carmela replied, for something to say.

"I hope so!" one of the housemaids exclaimed. "We finds it dismal being here with not much to do day after day, month after month. But as His Lordship's a young man, perhaps he'll be gettin' married."

As they spoke they looked at Carmela in a manner which made her think that they were visualising her as the Earl's bride.

Then she told herself that such an idea was ridiculous. After all, the Earl and Felicity were first cousins, and that was too close a relationship to be acceptable in most families.

"If he has a husband in mind for Felicity," Carmela told herself, "it will be another Gale who needs money, and I shall have to be very careful not to encourage anyone in case almost before I am aware of what is happening, I find myself married under false pretences!"

It was a frightening thought, but she was certain that she was upsetting herself unnecessarily even in considering it.

She knew it was fashionable to have long engagements, and in a month or two Jimmy's wife would be dead and then she would be free to disappear.

All the same, however calmly she tried to review the situation, however firmly she told herself there was no need to be agitated, her heart began to beat tumultuously as the housemaid exclaimed:

"We're here, M'Lady! Now you'll be able to see if you remember what a fine house Galeston is."

"As I was only five the last time I was here," Carmela replied, "I find it difficult to remember anything about it."

Nevertheless, when a few minutes later she saw that great house ahead of them, she thought that once they had seen it it would be impossible for anybody to forget such a magnificent building.

She had learnt from the Countess in the past that the house had originally been built on the site for a Cistercian Monastery, then altered, improved, and added to by every successive generation of Gales.

Felicity's grandfather in the last century had added a new facade to the house with high Corinthian columns and had bought statues and urns from Greece to ornament the top of the building.

The result was exceedingly impressive, and the house was so large that it made Carmela feel very small and insignificant and definitely apprehensive.

As if the horses which were pulling the very well-sprung carriage realised that they were home, they quickened their pace as they crossed the stone bridge over the lake with a swirl of wheels and drew up with a flourish outside the impressive front door.

There was a flight of steps leading up to it, and as the carriage arrived a red carpet was run down, and Carmela knew she was expected to walk on it to enter the house.

Feeling rather as if she were going to the guillotine, she stepped out of the carriage to see that the footmen in attendance wore powdered wigs with their elaborate livery, and each bowed to her politely as she passed them.

She smiled a little uncertainly in response, and on reaching the top of the steps she was greeted by the elderly Butler who looked like an Archbishop, and he said:

"Welcome home, M'Lady! It's a happy day for those of us who remember Your Ladyship to have you amongst us again."

"Thank you," Carmela replied. "I only wish my grandmother could be with me."

"That's what we all wishes, M'Lady, like it was in the good old days," the Butler said.

He led her through the great marble Hall with statues ornamenting it and some finely executed murals on the walls.

"His Lordship's expecting you, M'Lady. He'll join you in the Salon."

The Butler opened the door of a beautiful room hung with pictures, its windows looking out onto the garden filled with lilac and syringa.

"I will inform His Lordship of your arrival," the Butler said, then left her alone.

Carmela drew in her breath.

She found it difficult to take in much of the large room and instead walked to the window.

She had a sudden longing to be at home in the cottage with her father and to watch him paint one of his strange, mystical pictures. Nothing there would worry her except the problem of how to pay the bills they owed in the village.

Now that she was actually involved in this masquerade of deceiving the Earl into thinking she was Felicity, she thought that her position was not only perilous but exceedingly reprehensible.

How could she have agreed to act what was a lie when her mother had said a hundred times:

"Whoever we are, darling, it is a cowardly thing to evade the truth, and we should always be ready to face bravely whatever confronts us in life, however unpleasant."

"I am not lying for myself," Carmela protested to her conscience.

At the same time, she could not help feeling guilty, knowing that what she was doing, when it was exposed, would seem inexcusable.

She heard the door open and felt as if her heart had stopped beating. Then as she slowly turned round she saw the Earl walking towards her.

She was not quite certain how she had visualised him, but because Felicity hated him so violently and had described him in such venomous tones, she had expected someone grim and dark.

She was sure he would have a cruel face and in her mind he resembled the Roundheads whom she had always hated because they had beaten the Royalists.

Instead, the man advancing towards her was tall, slim, exceedingly handsome, and fashionably dressed.

At the same time, she was aware that he wore his clothes casually, as if they were not important, and she had the feeling that he would rather be attired in a uniform.

She could not think why she had such ideas, but as the Earl drew nearer and she saw him looking at her with what she thought were penetrating and critical eyes, she thought that after all he might be the ogre she had expected and Felicity had described.

"I am delighted to meet you, Cousin Felicity," the Earl said as he reached her side, and Carmela dropped him a curtsey.

She put out her hand as she did so, and as the Earl took it and she felt the strength of his fingers, she had the uncomfortable feeling that he was taking her captive and it would be difficult for her to escape from him.

"Have you had a good journey?" he asked.

"Yes, thank you," Carmela answered. "Your horses were very swift, and we did not linger on the way."

"Come and sit down," the Earl suggested, "and may I offer you some refreshment?"

"No, thank you."

"Luncheon will be ready in a short time. I am sure that you will wish to explore the place you have not seen for so many years."

"Yes, of course," Carmela agreed.

Because she was feeling shy, she was finding it difficult to look at the Earl.

But she was acutely conscious that his eyes were on her face and he seemed to be taking in not only her features but looking deep down inside her, as if already he suspected that she was not what she appeared to be.

Then she told herself she was being ridiculous.

She looked like Felicity, she was dressed like Felicity, and as none of the other Gales had seen her since she was five years old, why should they suspect for one moment that she was not who she said she was?

"I understand you are still in half-mourning for your grandmother," the Earl was saying. "I was not in England when she died, and it was only a month ago that I learnt you had been left alone."

Carmela did not speak. She merely inclined her head, thinking as she did so that that was when the Earl had learnt also of the vast fortune Felicity had been left.

Because he seemed to expect an answer, after a pause she replied in a low voice:

"I have been in France . . . staying with some of Grandmama's friends."

"In France?" the Earl questioned. "I learnt you were away from home, but I had not expected it to be abroad."

"Grandmama had French blood in her, and she had always wanted me to visit France, having very happy memories of it before the war."

"And what did you think of it now?" the Earl enquired.

"I loved the country and its people," Carmela answered evasively.

"They suffered greatly under Napoleon," he said. "We can only hope they will be able to reconstruct themselves as a nation and play their part in the restoration of Europe."

He spoke almost as if it mattered to him personally, and Carmela glanced at him, wanting to ask him a great deal more about France but feeling that it was a dangerous subject because she was actually so ignorant about it.

Instead she said:

"I have always heard how magnificent this house is, but it is even larger and more impressive than I expected."

The Earl smiled.

"That is what I felt too when I came back from Europe to take my place as head of the family."

He hesitated before he added:

"You realise that I am now your Guardian, Felicity, and as your Guardian I have plans for your future, which we will discuss later in the day. I am sure that now you would like to change before luncheon."

"Yes, of course," Carmela said, rising quickly to her feet.

The Earl walked beside her to the door and across the Hall to the foot of the stairs.

He glanced up and said:

"You will find the Housekeeper, Mrs. Humphries, who tells me she remembers your being born, waiting to show you to your room. I feel sure she will make you very comfortable."

"Thank you."

Carmela climbed the staircase, aware as she did so that she was glad to be leaving the Earl.

It was a comfort to be greeted effusively by Mrs. Humphries, who told her what a charming little girl she used to be and how much everybody on the Estate missed her grandmother.

"There's never been anybody like Her Ladyship," Mrs. Humphries said as she helped Carmela out of her travelling-clothes. "Like a Queen she looked, when there were parties here at Galeston. But there, I was only a young girl myself at the time and I thought the house itself was like a Palace."

"It is like one now!" Carmela said with a smile.

"We're only hoping His Lordship'll entertain and there'll be parties like there were in the old days," Mrs. Humphries said.

She went on to describe how sad and gloomy everything had been since the young Viscount had been killed in France, and her father had never recovered from the blow.

"His Lordship took it real bad, he did!" Mrs. Humphries said. "I used to wish you'd come back here to cheer him up. After all, M'Lady, you were his own flesh and blood, so to speak."

"I do not think it was ever suggested that I should come to him!" Carmela said.

She felt as if Mrs. Humphries was reproaching her for not being considerate towards her father. Then the Housekeeper replied:

"All this fighting amongst families is wrong, M'Lady, and that's a fact! It's bad enough when it's nation against nation, but when it's mother against son and the family is broken up, then it's not right, and nobody can tell me it is!"

"I quite agree with you," Carmela said.

"Well, now you're back, M'Lady, and although your father is not here, God rest his soul, I feel sure you'll help His Lordship as no-one else can do."

Carmela was inclined to say that His Lordship seemed perfectly self-sufficient and would have no need of help from anybody.

The more she thought about him, the more she was convinced that he was a frightening man, although not exactly in the way that Felicity had led her to expect.

It was just that she knew she had to be on her guard with him, and she felt too that he was sizing her up.

She had to admit it was natural for him to be suspicious of somebody who had been isolated from the family for so many years, but she did not like it.

When she had changed into another of Felicity's lovely gowns, this one white, with the only touch of mourning being the little mauve slippers she wore with it and a mauve ribbon to match in her hair, Mrs. Humphries escorted her to the top of the stairs.

"You look a picture, M'Lady, that you do!" she said. "Now you make up your mind to enjoy yourself there as much as we'll all enjoy having you. Then everybody'll be happy!"

As she spoke Mrs. Humphries glanced over the bannisters down to the Hall below, and Carmela had the idea that she was looking down apprehensively in case the Earl was listening to her.

'Even the servants are afraid of him!' she thought, and wondered why.

Then she went down the stairs, conscious of the elegance of her gown, of her new hair-style, and of the slight dusting of powder on her small nose.

As a footman hurried across the Hall to open the door of the Salon for her, she heard voices and realised that the Earl was not alone.

It was something she had not expected, and instinctively she braced herself to meet more strangers, hoping that if they were relations she would not make any mistake or say something that would give her away.

Then as she entered the Salon she saw that standing at the far end of it and talking to the Earl was a young man, very gorgeously arrayed and looking exactly as she expected a Dandy would appear.

His cravat was dazzlingly white, tied in a complicated and tricky fashion, the points of his collar high above the line of his chin.

His coat fitted so tightly that it was almost as if he had been poured into it, and the same applied to his champagne-coloured pantaloons.

His Hessian boots with gold laces were dazzling, and as he moved his hand, the sunlight from the windows glittered on a jewelled ring.

As she walked down the length of the room she realised that the Earl and his companion had ceased speaking and were watching her approach.

She reached the Earl and he said:

"Let me present, Sir, my cousin Felicity Gale— Royal Highness Prince Frederich von Horngelstein!"

With a start Carmela remembered to curtsey, and the Prince bowed as he said in excellent English:

"I am delighted to make your acquaintance, My Lady!"

"My cousin has not been here at Galeston since she was a child," the Earl explained, "and she is finding the house as impressive as I do."

"It must certainly be a change after the dilapidated and uncomfortable billets you occupied during the war," the Prince remarked.

"That was certainly true of Portugal," the Earl replied, "but in your country, Sir, I was extremely comfortable."

"Which was more than I was!" the Prince said with a laugh.

Now that she was near him Carmela could see that there was a very foreign look about him which should have told her that he was not English the moment she saw him.

She wondered why he was there, then as the two men went on talking, she gathered that while the Earl was with the Army of Occupation after the cessation of hostilities he had been in the Prince's country.

She hurriedly tried to remember when Horngelstein was, and she thought it must be one of the small German Principalities overrun by Napoleon, which as far as she remembered were, under the Treaty of Vienna, being given back their Royal status.

However, she felt very ignorant about the situation and was thankful that for the moment the Earl and the Prince were content to talk to each other and were making little effort to include her in the conversation.

That was not to say that the Prince was prepared to ignore her.

All through the meal that followed Carmela was aware that his eyes were continually on her face. He seemed to be "sizing her up" just as the Earl had done and, as she said to herself, to be enumerating her good points.

She could not gather exactly why the Prince was in England, but it was evident that he was on very good terms with the Earl, and occasionally the Prince spoke to him in terms of admiration and, Carmela thought, of gratitude.

'The Earl has obviously helped the Prince to rein-state himself in his country,' she thought perceptively.

She decided that as soon as she had the opportunity she would find an Atlas to learn something about a country of which she knew nothing.

She thought the luncheon was excellent, and they were waited on by a large number of footmen.

The silver on the table was magnificent, and the Dining-Room itself was an extremely impressive room, hung with portraits of the Gale ancestors painted by famous artists.

'I wish Papa were with me,' Carmela thought to herself.

She knew he would be able not only to recognise most of the pictures but also to tell her amusing little anecdotes concerning the artists.

She remembered how he had once said to her when they were talking about pictures:

"What I would like to do is to take you with me to Florence or to Rome."

Carmela thought now she would be only too happy

to have him here with her, as she knew from what the
Countess had said that the Gales had a very fine
collection of pictures not only by English but also by
French and Dutch Masters.

She was thinking of her father when the Earl
unexpectedly said:

"You look very serious, Felicity. Is anything
worrying you?"

"No, indeed," Carmela replied. "I was thinking of
your pictures."

"When I get back the collection stolen by Napoleon and taken to Paris," the Prince said before the Earl
could speak, "I think you will find them not only
beautiful but containing some very fine examples of
mediaeval art that will be interesting to you."

"All pictures interst me," Carmela replied. "You
say your collection was stolen... will there be any
difficulty in getting it back now that the war is over?"

"That is what I am trying to find out," the Prince
replied, "and I need His Lordship's help to make sure I
am not cheated by the French Government."

"I have already spoken to the Duke of Wellington
about your problem," the Earl said, "and he has promised
me he will do everything in his power to see that
justice is done."

"That is all I ask," the Prince replied, "and I think,
My Lady, you will agree that justice is something we
are all entitled to after the horrors and privations of
war."

"Of course," Carmela agreed. "I hope Your Royal
Highness will be fortunate in your quest."

"With your help I will make sure of it," the Prince
replied.

Carmela looked at him wide-eyed. She felt she
could not have heard him aright.

Then she supposed that he was in fact only expecting
her to support her cousin in finding his treasures and
having them returned to their rightful country.

When luncheon was ended they moved not to the

Salon but to a large, impressive Library. The Prince made an excuse to leave, and the Earl and Carmela were left alone.

Carmela was not attending to what was being said but was looking round the Library with delight.

She felt there was so much here she wanted to read. The first book she needed was an Atlas, which she hoped would be quite easy to find.

Therefore, as the door closed behind the Prince, she said to the Earl:

"As I am lamentably ignorant as to where His Royal Highness's country is, do you think I could find an Atlas among this magnificent collection of books?"

"I am sure there is one," the Earl replied. "I will see if I can find the catalogue."

As he spoke he walked towards a table on which there were some books and papers, saying as he did so:

"I am delighted to learn that you are interested in Horngelstein."

"I am interested to know where it is and what sort of people live there. I presume from the name they speak German."

"Horngelstein is on the border of Germany and France, and the people are half-German and half-French," the Earl replied. "You will find them charming, anxious to be friendly, and very happy that the war has ended."

"Like a great many other people," Carmela remarked.

The Earl was turning over the papers on the table, then at last he exclaimed:

"Oh, here is the catalogue! I thought there must be one, although the last Curator has retired."

He looked up what he wanted in the catalogue, then handed Carmela a book covered in red leather. She set it down on the flat-topped writing-table which was almost in the centre of the room and opened it.

She turned over the pages until she came to a map depicting Europe, and the Earl pointed to a small country low down on the border of France and said:

"That is Horngelstein. Your future country!"

Carmela was very still. Then she asked after a moment:

"D-did you say . . . *my* country?"

"I thought you would have guessed by now why the Prince is here."

Carmela raised her eyes to the Earl's face as she said:

"I . . . I do not . . . understand what you are . . . saying to me."

"Then let me make it clear," the Earl replied. "As your Guardian I have arranged for you to marry—in fact a very brilliant match from your point of view—His Royal Highness Prince Frederich!"

Carmela felt her anger rising.

"You have arranged . . . this without . . . asking for my . . . permission to do so?"

"I cannot believe you would object."

She thought there was a note of genuine surprise in the Earl's voice, and she said quickly:

"But of course I object! Can you believe that I, or any other woman, would want to marry a man she had never met before and has talked to for only a few minutes?"

The Earl stared at her as if he could not believe what she was saying. Then he said:

"I never imagined you would not be delighted to be a reigning Princess."

"Why ever should you think that?" Carmela answered. "Although you may not be aware of it, women have feelings like everybody else!"

For a moment the Earl seemed to have difficulty in finding words in which to express himself. Then he said:

"I may have been mistaken, but I always understood that young girls had their marriages arranged for them by their parents, and that they accepted what was proposed without argument."

Carmela was uncomfortably aware that this was more or less the truth.

Jimmy Salwick had been pressurised into marriage when he was young because his and the bride's parents had thought it advantageous for them both, and there had been no question of their being in love with each other.

She remembered too that Felicity had talked of her friends who had been married to men for whom they had a positive aversion, and they had not been able to avoid it.

Now she understood that Felicity had been afraid to come to Galeston just because this sort of thing could happen, and as the Earl was her Guardian, there would have been nothing she could do to prevent it.

Carmela knew she must fight not only because she was not the heiress the Earl believed her to be, but also because her father and mother had encouraged her to think for herself.

Even if the Prince had really wanted to marry Carmela Lyndon, a girl of no consequence, she would not accept him or any other man in such a high-handed manner.

She thought now that Felicity had been absolutely right in saying that the Gales were ruthless and dominating.

Although it was not a Gale whom she was expected to marry, she was certain from what had been said at luncheon that the Prince needed money desperately for his country, which had been ravaged by war.

That was why the Earl was arranging his marriage to a very wealthy young woman.

Carmela knew that the Earl was staring at her in a puzzled manner, and if she had not been in such an uncomfortable situation it might almost have been amusing.

"Perhaps," he conceded after a moment, "I should have broken this to you more gently. But let me assure you that the Prince is a very charming man whom I know well. He has suffered the humiliation and misery of having his country overrun by the French, his Palace pilfered, and other unpleasant incidents such as always happen in wartime."

"I presume he is also in need of money!"

"Of course," the Earl agreed, "and I can imagine no better way of spending your vast fortune, Felicity, than by assisting this charming and able young man and making his people happy."

Carmela did not speak for a moment and he went on:

"The country needs Schools and Hospitals, and Churches have to be rebuilt. I am certain you would find it of absorbing interest."

"To be married to a man I do not know?" Carmela enquired.

"I have told you he is charming."

"That may be your opinion," she said, "but you do not have to live with him in a strange country surrounded by strangers."

"I am sure you will soon make friends with the Prince and his countrymen," the Earl replied patiently.

"Perhaps, if I really wished to," Carmela retorted. "But let me make it very clear, My Lord, that I have no intention of marrying at the moment, and certainly not a foreign Prince whom I met only an hour ago!"

The Earl put the catalogue down on the table with a slam and walked towards her.

"This is ridiculous, Felicity!" he said. "I consider it very wrong of you to take up this attitude. I have already apologised for being slightly precipitate, but you must be well aware that you have to be married sooner or later, and I have no wish to see you pursued by fortune-hunters."

"What else is the Prince?"

She was too angry at the moment to feel frightened.

She was thinking how fortunate it was that Felicity was on her way to France with Jimmy and was not here to fight frantically against the Earl, who she could see was growing angry too.

There was an expression in his eyes and a squareness of his chin that told her that he was as obstinate and determined as she had always been told the Gales were when opposed.

She and the Earl stood defying each other, and because he was so tall and broad-shouldered and towered above her, Carmela could not help feeling rather overwhelmed.

But because she knew she was in the fortunate position of being not Felicity but her poor, poverty-stricken self, she could fight for what she believed were the right principles in the whole argument, knowing that when it came to a real "show-down" the Prince would not wish to marry her because she actually had no money.

"It is, in my opinion," she said, "absolutely wrong that any woman should be sold over the counter as if she were a piece of merchandise. As I have already said, we have feelings, and I personally would not marry any man, however important he might be, unless I . . . loved him and . . . he loved me."

"You astound me!" the Earl said. "And if it comes to that, how are you ever to know, with your fortune, whether a man loves you for yourself or for your money?"

Carmela was silent for a moment. Then she said:

"I think that love . . . real love . . . would be impossible to disguise or pretend! And unless one was very stupid one would not be taken in by compliments that were prompted only by greed, or loving words that were . . . insincere."

Because for the moment he could not think of an answer, the Earl walked away from her towards the window to stand looking out onto the Park.

After a long silence he said:

"I suppose that because I am very ignorant of

young women, having never had much to do with them, I never anticipated for a moment that you would not accept my decision that this was in your best interests. In fact, I believed I was doing you a favour."

"A favour which is actually an insult to my intelligence!"

"I always believed that when they came out of the School-Room, girls were gauche and nit-witted," the Earl said, "but you are obviously neither of those things!"

"You never met my grandmother, but you must have heard of her," Carmela replied. "The old servants here have never forgotten her, and I can assure you that living with her was better than being educated at any of the finest Universities."

The Earl gave a short laugh.

"Now I begin to understand why the relations with whom I have been in contact since I inherited have always referred to the quarrel between your father and his mother as if it were a world-shattering epic."

"That is what it must have been to them. She left here vowing she would never return, and she made a life for herself elsewhere."

"As you went with her, I presume you will grow up to be as awe-inspiring and determined as she was!" the Earl remarked.

"I sincerely hope so," Carmela replied.

As she spoke she thought how much she had admired and loved the Countess. It was the absolute truth to say that being with her was an education in itself, and both she and Felicity had been very lucky in knowing such a remarkable woman.

There was silence. Then the Earl said:

"You are only eighteen, Felicity. However well educated you may be, your grandmother is dead, and as I am now your Guardian you will have to obey me."

"And if I refuse to do so?"

"Then I shall have to find means, which I have no

wish to do, to force you to acknowledge my authority."

Carmela smiled scornfully.

"What are you suggesting?" she asked. "Locking me up in the dungeon, if the house has one? Starving or beating me into submission? Or simply dragging me screaming to the altar?"

She spoke mockingly, and because her voice was very soft and musical it did not sound as aggressive as it might have done.

There was silence. Then the Earl said:

"I think it is rather easier than that. I believe that as your Guardian I have the use of your money and the spending of it until you are twenty-one."

Carmela thought frantically that if this was so, he might be able to prevent Felicity from drawing on her Bank Accounts, and it would be difficult to warn her that this might happen.

She tried to think of what she could do or what she could say, but she had the feeling that the Earl, having had the last word, was aware of her discomfiture and was gloating over it.

'I hate him!' she thought.

At the same time, she knew he had out-witted her for the moment and she must be very, very careful not to do Felicity any harm.

There was silence for a long time, then at last the Earl turned from the window and came back towards her.

"I think, Felicity," he said, "we are both being rather precipitate in drawing our daggers so quickly and fighting each other without a thought as to who might be injured in the process."

Carmela looked at him but did not speak, and he said:

"Shall we start again? I will apologise for acting too quickly and ask you instead to consider my proposition without committing yourself one way or the other."

Carmela was well aware that while he was conced-

ing her a small victory, at the same time the battle was
by no means over, and she was quite certain that he had
every intention of being the victor in the end.

However, because it was an olive-branch which she
thought it wise to accept, she said in a low voice:

"It is true that you took me by surprise, but if I
can, as you suggest, consider this proposition and get to
know the Prince a great deal better than I do at the
moment . . . perhaps I shall come to think . . . differently."

As she finished speaking she thought that the Earl
was smiling in a self-satisfied way.

"At the same time," she said quickly, "you will
understand that as Grandmama has not been dead for
very long and I am still in mourning for her, it would be
impossible for me to think of being married for some
months."

There was a frown on the Earl's forehead, and she
realised that he had not thought of this before, any
more than she had until this very minute.

"I cannot believe," he said after a second or so,
"that your grandmother would wish you to mourn
unnecessarily long."

"I think how long one mourns depends more on
what one's feelings are than on what is laid down in the
social code," Carmela replied in a deceptively soft
voice.

"I can understand that," the Earl agreed. "At the
same time, Felicity, I want you to think of the good
you can do with your fortune, the people who will
benefit by your generosity, and what I genuinely
believe will be the happiness you will find with a very
remarkable and delightful young man."

"I will certainly think about it," Carmela answered.

The Earl held out his hand.

"That is all I want to hear," he said. "In the
meantime, shall we try to be friends? We really cannot
start another war amongst the Gales."

Because there was nothing else she could do,

Carmela put her hand in his, and once again she was conscious of the strength of his fingers.

At the same time, she felt that he was drawing her, compelling her, and she would have to fight to resist him.

Chapter Four

Coming down the stairs for dinner dressed in a beautiful gown, Carmela thought that if she were not so frightened of doing something which might have repercussions on Felicity, the situation would actually be rather amusing.

Because the Earl had called a truce, he was going out of his way to be charming and to treat her like an intelligent woman instead of a brainless School-girl.

For the last two days she had realised the effort he was making, and she felt it was perhaps the first time in his life that he had had to consider a woman's feelings rather than his own.

Now he included her in any conversation he had with the Prince and asked her opinion and even listened to what she had to say.

She was quite certain that what he normally expected was to lay down the law and have everybody obey him.

However, protocol and good manners compelled him to defer to the Prince, although it was obvious that the younger man had so much admiration for him that it amounted almost to adoration.

Therefore, Carmela was left to balance the situation, and when she could be herself without being afraid of involving Felicity, she began to enjoy the cut and thrust of the dialogues she had with the Earl, which were almost as if they fenced with each other.

71

She knew that she surprised him with her knowledge of art, for in fact she knew more about pictures than he did.

What astonished him even more was that she also had a good grasp of the political situation in Europe.

This she owed not to her father, who of course had taught her about art, but to the Countess, who because of her long acquaintance with Statesmen and Politicians had always been interested in everything that was happening not only abroad but in Parliament at home.

Every day Carmela and Felicity had been made to read aloud the Members' speeches which were reported in *The Times* and *The Morning Post*.

The Countess would then explain to them what they did not understand, and because she knew so many of the speakers, she would also give them a "thumb-nail sketch" of the Political Leaders on both sides of the House.

Felicity had found it rather boring, but to Carmela it was always extremely interesting, and she used her knowledge now to surprise and, she knew, bewilder the Earl.

"Why should he think all young girls are stupid?" she asked herself indignantly, and set out to prove that he had no grounds for thinking so.

Last night when they had had a spirited argument about the reforms that were sadly overdue to improve the lot of the farming community, the Earl had said:

"I may have been out of England for a long time, but I cannot believe that things are as bad as you say they are."

"Unfortunately, they are even worse," Carmela replied. "Cheap food from Europe is now beginning to flood the market, and it looks like the farmers in England are about to go bankrupt."

She saw by the expression on the Earl's face that he did not believe her, and she added:

"Ask how many Country Banks closed their doors

last year, and if you talk to your tenant farmers rather than to those you employ, you will find they are fighting desperately to keep their heads above water."

The Earl was silent for a moment. Then he said:

"I thought young ladies like yourself were too busy dancing to know about the sufferings of the labouring class."

"We can still see with our eyes and hear with our ears," Carmela replied. "In the same way, Your Lordship might look at the condition of men who were crippled in the war and see how they are faring in a country that has given them no pension since they were dismissed from the Services and apparently expects them to live by begging in the streets."

Because she was angry at the sufferings she had seen even in Huntingdonshire and had read in reports in the newspapers, she spoke aggressively and her eyes flashed in a way which the Earl thought was extremely attractive.

He glanced at the Prince, hoping that he was not only listening to Carmela but admiring her, and realised he was looking down at his plate and crumbling a piece of bread absent-mindedly as he did so.

"What is worrying you, Sir?" the Earl asked.

The Prince started, as if his thoughts were far away. The he replied after a pause:

"I was thinking that if these things are occurring in a rich, prosperous country like England, what must be happening in Horngelstein?"

There was silence and Carmela knew the Earl was thinking that the answer to this question was that soon he would have Lady Felicity's fortune to expend for the benefit of his subjects in need.

Because this was a dangerous topic, she said quickly:

"Let us talk of something more amusing for His Royal Highness. I am sure he should really be in London at this time of the year, attending the parties which the Prince Regent is giving at Carlton House."

"Have you ever been to one?" the Prince asked.

Carmela shook her head.

"I was to have been presented to the Queen this year at Buckingham Palace," she replied, "if my grandmother had not died."

"That must have been very disappointing for you."

"It was far more disastrous to lose my grandmother, who was a very remarkable person."

She glanced at the Earl from under her eye-lashes and said provocatively:

"She was clever, besides having too much personality for the Gale family! However, they will never know how much they missed in losing her for all those years after she left here."

"You can hardly blame me for that," the Earl said in an amused tone.

"Grandmama always said the Gales were obstinate, dogmatic, and very reluctant to see anybody else's point of view but their own."

The Earl laughed.

"Is that what you think of me?"

"I would not be so impolite to my host as to accuse. him of any of those characteristics," Carmela said demurely. "But of course you are a Gale!"

"And so are you," he retorted.

"There is always a black sheep in every flock."

"Is that what you would call yourself?" he challenged. "I can think of much more flattering descriptions."

"And so can I," the Prince interposed. "You are very beautiful, Lady Felicity, as I expect dozens of men have told you."

His words sounded too smooth to be sincere, and Carmela looking at him knew that he admired her, but she was also sure that he was not in the least enamoured of her.

As she thought about it, she had the feeling that often when he appeared to be engrossed in the conversation and was even paying her compliments, some part of him was elsewhere, and she was determined to find out if she was right.

The opportunity came after dinner when the gentlemen joined her in the Salon, then almost immediately the Earl was called away.

The Butler had come and said something in his ear, whereupon he rose, murmured his apologies, and followed the servant from the room.

"I wonder what has happened," Carmela remarked.

"Does it matter?" the Prince asked.

Carrying a glass of brandy in his hand, he sat down beside her on the sofa and said:

"Now I can talk to you. I sometimes feel as if our host, admirable though he is, is much too efficient a chaperone."

"Surely we have nothing to say to each other that the Earl could not overhear."

"That is not true," the Prince contradicted. "I would prefer to talk to you alone, Lady Felicity, and it is very difficult to make love to you in the presence of an audience."

Carmela quickly looked away from him.

"That is something I do not wish to hear," she said. "We have only . . . just met, Your Royal Highness . . . and as you are doubtless aware . . . although I would like to be your friend . . . there is no question of . . . anything else between us."

She spoke hesitatingly because she was choosing her words with care, and after a moment the Prince said:

"You know that your Guardian has agreed that you should marry me?"

"So he told me, and I informed him that I would not marry a man unless I was in love with him."

The Prince put his glass of brandy down on the small table by the side of the sofa, then bent forward to take Carmela's hand in his.

She stiffened because she did not like his touching her, and he said:

"Both I and my country need you as my wife."

"What you are really saying," Carmela replied, "is that you need my . . . fortune to repair the ravages of war."

She thought the Prince might be offended and went on quickly:

"It is a very great honour that Your Highness should wish to marry me . . . at the same time, because I am an ordinary English girl, I want to marry someone I love and who . . . loves me."

"And you do not think you would come to love me when we know each other better?" the Prince asked.

"That might possibly happen," Carmela agreed, "but I cannot help feeling, and I know Your Highness will forgive me if I am wrong, that your heart is already given elsewhere."

It was a bold venture, but at the same time Carmela was almost certain she was right and that the Prince was often thinking wistfully of somebody who was not present.

At her words he started, and instead of dropping her hand his fingers tightened on them almost as if he needed her support.

"Why should you say that?" he asked.

"I just feel that you are thinking of somebody else," she replied, "and that she means a great deal to you."

The Prince gave a deep sigh.

"You are—how do you say?—clairvoyant!"

"Then it is true?"

He nodded.

"And it is impossible for you to marry her?" Carmela asked softly.

The Prince sighed again.

"That is what I want to do," he said, "but to tell the truth, I am a coward."

"A coward?" Carmela questioned.

Again his fingers seemed to grip her hand as if he drew strength from her, before he said:

"She means everything in the world to me! But she is—French!"

There was a little pause. Then Carmela said:

"I understand. After what your country has suffered from Napoleon Bonaparte, your people would not willingly accept a Princess who is of that nationality."

"I think perhaps they might do so in time," the Prince said, "and if there was no alternative."

Carmela felt that she understood.

"What Your Royal Highness is saying," she said, "is that when my cousin suggested that you needed a rich wife, you did not dare to tell him you had any other ideas."

"You understand," the Prince murmured.

"Of course I understand," Carmela said, "and you must be brave and marry the woman you love and not be pressurised into taking a wife who has been chosen for you by somebody else."

"It is difficult for me not to do what has been suggested first by your cousin, who was commanding the Army of Occupation in my country, and also by the Council of Ministers in Vienna," the Prince said.

"They may think they have the solution to your problems on paper," Carmela answered. "But for a country to be happy, it is necessary for the man who rules over it to be happy too."

"If only I could believe that," the Prince said.

"Will you tell me about this lady whom you love?" Carmela asked softly.

"Her father is a distinguished Frenchman who lived in France just at the border with Horngelstein. Until Napoleon became the Emperor and started to dominate the whole of Europe, we were happy with both the French and the other countries to the north and east of us."

"That is something which will happen again now that Napoleon is defeated and a prisoner on St. Helena," Carmela said.

"I am sure you are right," the Prince agreed, "but in the meantime your cousin, when he came to rescue us from the last pockets of opposition maintained by Napoleon's Troops, not only put me back on the throne but promised every help he could give me in reconstructing our industries and relieving the most poverty-stricken of my subjects."

Carmela thought how much the Earl would enjoy reorganising the whole country and setting it, as he thought, to rights, but aloud she said:

"I have always found that people who think they know what is best for us are somewhat overbearing, and if we have any character at all, we have to decide things for ourselves when they matter personally."

"That is what I have wanted to do," the Prince said in a low voice, "but Gabrielle told me I must think of Horngelstein and forget her."

"If she said that," Carmela said, "then I am sure she really loves you."

"Do you think so?" the Prince asked eagerly.

"But of course!" Carmela replied. "If a woman really loves a man with her whole heart, she tries to do what is right for him, whatever the sacrifice for herself."

As she spoke she was sure that for any woman, especially one who was French, a race always very conscious of rank and title, to give up a throne could mean only one thing—Gabrielle loved the Prince too much to hurt him.

'It is what I would feel myself,' Carmela thought, and she went on:

"What you must do is to go back to the woman you love and ask her if she is brave enough to face those of your countrymen who will still be hostile to France, and help you to set things to rights in your own way."

"They will come to love her as I do," the Prince said. "I am sure of that."

"As some of your subjects have French blood in them," Carmela said, "I am sure it will not be as difficult as you think it will be!"

She paused before she continued:

"I have read in the newspapers that Europe is desperately short of all sorts of materials, implements, tools, and other necessities which were not manufactured during the war because every effort was directed to producing weapons."

"That is true," the Prince agreed.

"There must be many things that you could make in Horngelstein," Carmela suggested. "I am sure if you ask for a loan from England or from those who are trying to reorganise European affairs in Vienna, they would give you one to enable you at least to start the wheels turning and your people working."

The Prince lifted her hand to his lips.

"Thank you, thank you!" he said. "You have given me new heart, and now, thanks to you, I will try to behave like a man."

He gave a deep sigh as if a burden had fallen from his shoulders as he said:

"I am ashamed that I listened when your cousin tempted me with the suggestion that a very rich wife would solve all my problems. He said he would find one for me and made it sound so easy and so plausible that I thought I was doing the right thing in sacrificing myself and my own feelings for the good of my country. Now I realise I was just being weak, and what you would call—inefficient."

Carmela gave a little laugh.

She was thinking of how the Countess had always said that when the Gales were determined about something they let nothing and nobody stand in their way.

"What has really happened," she said, "is that you have been listening to the smooth talk of a salesman who is absolutely convinced that his goods are the best, but has not really given you the chance to express your own needs."

The Prince laughed.

"I think you are being unkind to your cousin. At the same time, he is rather overpowering."

"All the Gales are the same."

"Except you," the Prince said, "and I find you not only adorable but inspiring."

Once again he took Carmela's hand and kissed it and said:

"Thank you, thank you! I think you are very beautiful, one of the most attractive women I have ever met, and I want you to meet my Gabrielle."

"I shall be very delighted to do so," Carmela replied.

"We will reconstruct my country together," the Prince said with a light in his eyes and a note of joy in his voice that had not been there before, "and when you come to stay with us, Lady Felicity, you will be astounded at what we have achieved!"

"I am sure I shall," Carmela replied with a laugh.

Then as if the Prince suddenly remembered the Earl, he looked nervously towards the door before he said:

"What am I to say to your cousin? If I have to tell him that I have changed my mind, he will be very angry and perhaps insulted."

Carmela thought for a moment. Then she said:

"Can you not tell him you have received a communication from your Chancellor or your Prime Minister asking you to return immediately to Horngelstein because there is a crisis of some sort?"

The Prince did not speak, but he was listening and Carmela went on:

"You can tell him you will only be going away for a few days, perhaps a week. But in fact you must immediately go and see the lady you love and make arrangements for your wedding."

As she spoke Carmela gave a little cry and clasped her hands together.

"Do you not see," she said, "that a Royal wedding, whoever the bride may be, will excite and cheer up the people of your country when they are feeling low and depressed after the privations of wartime."

She smiled as she went on:

"The women will all want new gowns in which to celebrate such a romantic event, and if you tell them eloquently how much you love your future wife, I know that whatever her nationality they will want you to be happy."

As she spoke she thought that the mere fact that the Prince was in love would evoke a response in all the young people, especially the women. If he and Gabrielle handled the situation diplomatically, they would soon overcome any opposition there might be to their marriage.

"You are right, I am sure you are right!" the Prince said fervently.

He thought for a moment, then he said:

"As it happens I did receive some letters today. A courier brought them down from our Embassy in London, but they were not of any particular importance."

"The Earl is not to know that."

Carmela thought again before she said:

"You could say that you did not want to spoil the evening by telling him this earlier. And then, to prevent him from suspecting anything, you could go on to tell him that you have had an interesting conversation with me while we were alone, and I have promised that we will have a further talk on the position between us when you return."

It took a moment for the Prince to assimilate exactly what she was saying. Then he smiled and his eyes twinkled.

"That is very diplomatic, Lady Felicity," he said, "and will allay any suspicion the Earl may have as to why I am going back."

"Yes, of course," Carmela said. "It would be a mistake to let him think you are running away."

The Prince laughed, and it was a very young, boyish sound.

"You are magnificent! Perhaps after all I am making a great mistake in not insisting that you marry me and rule over my country in the manner of Catherine the Great!"

"There is nothing you would dislike more!" Carmela said. "And I am sure, without meaning to flatter Your Royal Highness, that you will be a very good and popular Monarch."

"Thank you," the Prince said, "thank you! It is difficult for me to tell you what you have done for me and how different I feel about the future."

"You will think I am being clairvoyant again when I tell you that you will be very happy with your Gabrielle," Carmela said, "and that together you will make Horngelstein a very prosperous country."

"I hope so! I sincerely hope so!" the Prince replied. "I shall strive by every means in my power to make your words come true."

As he was speaking he was holding Carmela's hands in both of his and thanking her with a sincerity which she knew came from the very bottom of his heart.

She was smiling at him and he at her when the door opened and the Earl came in.

Because she was facing in that direction she saw him before the Prince did and was aware that he must have noticed their position on the sofa and that their hands were linked.

She was sure that he would put the wrong construction on it and she could see an expression of satisfaction on his face as he walked towards them.

The Prince released Carmela's hand and rose to his feet.

"I have just been telling Lady Felicity, My Lord," he said, "the disappointing news that I have to return to Horngelstein for a few days."

"You are leaving us?" the Earl asked.

"It is something that indeed I have no wish to do,"
the Prince went on, "but I have had a letter from my
Prime Minister this morning, begging me to return to
settle a small constitutional crisis which concerns the
throne."

He sighed realistically before he added:

"It is something which necessitates my personal
attention but will not take long. I hope to be back
within a week."

There had been a frown on the Earl's forehead, but
now it vanished as he said:

"I shall miss you, Sir, and I very much hope you
will hurry back as quickly as possible."

"As I was telling the lovely Lady Felicity," the
Prince said, "it is something I am very eager to do."

He smiled at Carmela in a flirtatious manner which
made her want to laugh.

Instead, she said in a commiserative tone:

"It is so tiresome for Your Royal Highness, but
from all I hear it is now much easier than it was to
travel through France, especially at this time of the
year."

"That is true," the Prince agreed, "and if I leave
first thing tomorrow morning I shall hope to be back
here at the end of next week."

"We will be looking forward to your return," Carmela
said, "will we not, Cousin Selwyn?"

"Yes, indeed," the Earl replied. "I will arrange for
my fastest horses to carry you to Dover, where my
yacht will be ready to take you across the Channel. This
will be far quicker than if you have to wait for the
ordinary ships that now make the crossing, I believe,
twice a day."

"You are very kind," the Prince said. "It is really
impossible to express my gratitude for all you have
done for me."

"Then please do not try," the Earl said hastily. "I

will go and make arrangements for your journey, and as
you suggest, it would be wise for you to leave early."

He walked towards the door as he spoke, and
immediately he was out of earshot the Prince said
to Carmela:

"It worked! It really worked!"

"Of course," she replied, "but be very careful not
to arouse in any way his suspicions that you are not
intending to return."

"No, of course not," the Prince agreed.

Then as if the thought struck him he asked:

"Will you tell him after I have gone that I will not
be coming back?"

"Not unless I have to," Carmela replied. "I have
no wish for his wrath to fall on my head until it is
completely unavoidable."

"He has been very kind and helpful," the Prince
said. "I dislike having to deceive him. At the same
time..."

"Your future is yours, not his," Carmela interposed
before he could finish the sentence.

As she spoke she thought it would do the Earl a lot
of good for his plan to go awry.

"He is far too busy interfering in other people's
affairs," she told herself.

She thought again how fortunate it was that she
could lose nothing by defying the Earl and how very
different it might have been for Felicity if, in ignorance
that the Prince's heart was elsewhere, she had been
forced into marrying him.

'It was lucky I guessed,' Carmela thought, and she
knew that her perception, or her clairvoyance, as the
Prince had called it, was something she had been born
with. It was an instinct, or perhaps a talent, that
Felicity did not have.

'Well, the Prince will be happy,' she thought, 'and
I can play for time until Felicity is married.'

She and the Prince talked of other things until the

Earl returned, and once again as he came in through the door and saw their heads together he was bound to think that his plans were going smoothly and they were becoming attached to each other.

Only when the Prince had said good-night and gone to his own room to make sure, as he said, that everything was packed to his satisfaction, were Carmela and the Earl alone together.

"It is extremely annoying," he remarked, "that Prince Frederick should have to leave us just when I thought you two were getting along so well together."

"He is a handsome young man," Carmela said, "and more intelligent than I suspected."

"That sounds a very pompous remark from a girl of your age," the Earl said scathingly.

"You have funny ideas about age," Carmela replied. "May I point out, as you do not seem to be aware of it, that there is no yard-stick by which one can measure people's intelligence, since year by year they develop in different ways."

"I am aware of that," the Earl said.

"Then you should also be aware that some women at thirty are nothing but frivolous, empty-headed fools, while a girl even of my age can sometimes have an intelligent thought in her head."

The Earl laughed.

"When you snarl at me like a small tiger-cat," he said, "your eyes flash sparks of fire and I am dazzled by your ferocity."

"I am sorry if it is something that disconcerts you."

"On the contrary, I find it intriguing," the Earl replied, "just as it obviously intrigues our Royal guest also. But now that he is leaving us, I have to make a decision as to what to do about you until he returns."

"There are horses to ride, and much of the Estate I have still not seen," Carmela said.

"I am in a similar position," the Earl answered, "but what I am really asking is if you wish to be entertained by members of the family, who will be only too eager and curious to make your acquaintance, or by my neighbours, who I believe have called on me but whom I have not yet met."

Because she thought that would be dangerous, Carmela said quickly and insistently:

"Oh, please let us be alone! I have no wish at the moment to be cross-questioned about Grandmama by other members of her family, and as the weather is so lovely you surely do not wish to sit indoors making polite chit-chat to folk who will be extremely curious about you."

"God forbid!" the Earl said fervently. "And now that I think about it, they might consider it very strange that you are staying here without being chaperoned by some elderly relative."

Carmela knew they would think it even stranger if they were aware that she was not who she pretended to be.

Because she thought an elderly Chaperone would be a tremendous bore, she said quickly:

"Quite frankly, I imagine you are in the same position as if I were staying here with my father, and even the Gales could not object to that!"

The Earl laughed.

"The way you say 'even the Gales' tells me exactly what you think about them."

"I know what they thought about Grandmama," Carmela flashed.

"It was certainly no worse than what she thought about them," the Earl said. "I can only hope that you will not think the same."

"As you are the only Gale I have met so far, I will let you know my feelings when they become clarified in my mind."

"You are making me apprehensive!" the Earl said mockingly.

"I am not breaking our truce," Carmela said quickly.

"I should hope not," he replied. "Besides, I am content as things are, and very hopeful of what may be."

Carmela knew he was referring to the Prince, and because she thought it would lull him into a sense of security, she looked down in what she hoped was a coy, shy manner, her eye-lashes very dark against her pale cheeks.

There was silence, then while she was wondering what the Earl was thinking, he suddenly said:

"You are very beautiful, Felicity, and with the incredible fortune you possess, the Prince is a fool to leave now, without your promise in his pocket."

"It will not be for very long," Carmela said after a moment.

"I know," the Earl replied. "At the same time, I suppose I am afraid that the Archangel Gabriel may drop down out of the sky and carry you away, or there may be another even more advantageous offer for your hand, which I would find it hard to reject."

Carmela laughed.

"I think it is unlikely, My Lord, that the Archangel Gabriel will appear. But perhaps Apollo might offer me a seat in his chariot as he rides across the sky, and I would certainly find it hard to refuse him."

"Apollo's horses are no faster than mine," the Earl boasted, "and I will promise the Prince they will be waiting for him at Dover on his return, so that you will not have a chance to escape him."

"You sound as if you are certain I shall try."

"You are deliberately provoking me into saying I shall shut you up and keep you my prisoner," the Earl remarked.

"That would be an unusual experience," Carmela answered, "and will undoubtedly depend on who the gaoler might be."

She looked up at the Earl to see his reaction as they duelled once again with each other.

Then incredibly she was aware with a perception

which could not be denied that he thought she was
flirting with him.

*   *   *

The next morning, Carmela realised as she awoke
that she was thinking of the Earl in the same way as she
had when she had gone to sleep.

She had chuckled to herself then, because it had
seemed to her absolutely absurd that the Earl should
for one moment think that she was trying to attract
him.

The idea had never been in her mind, but she
supposed it was not an unreasonable one, considering
that despite his overwhelming personality he was in fact
a very presentable and attractive man.

"How could he think, how could he imagine for
one moment, that his cousin Felicity would think about
him in such a way?" Carmela asked herself.

Then she told herself that if the Earl could imagine
that she was considering him as a man, it would make
him more eager than he was already to marry her off
and get her out of the way.

She was well aware what sort of woman the Earl
found attractive, and from all he had said it was quite
obvious that it would not be a young girl.

When Carmela thought it over, she decided that it
was really insulting that he should expect to find her a
complacent nit-wit who would carry out his instructions
immediately he gave them without having a thought in
her head, or being able to express herself only by
saying "yes" to everything he suggested.

When she thought back over the conversations of
the last few days, she realised that he had been unable
to hide his surprise whenever she said anything intelligent or argued with him in a manner which made him
exert his own brain.

It would be a very good thing, she thought, if she
could teach him a lesson in some way which would stop
him from being so opinionated in the future.

As she thought it over, she knew that it would indeed be a lesson when he learnt that the Prince would not return and intended to marry the Frenchwoman Gabrielle, about whom presumably the Earl had never heard.

'It will certainly surprise him, especially when I tell him that I knew the truth all along,' Carmela thought with satisfaction.

She wished she had not to wait for so long before she could score off the Earl and make him realise that he had been wrong in planning to marry her off to suit his own ends.

'I daresay he has been commended for his admirable powers of organisation when he was in the Army,' she thought scornfully, and wondered exactly what he had put in his reports to the Duke of Wellington.

"Well, he was wrong! Wrong! Wrong!" she told herself. "Just as he was wrong about Felicity! And he was not prepared to listen when I tried to argue with him about it."

Dressed in her riding-habit, she went downstairs, looking as she went at the portraits of the Gale ancestors on the wall, who seemed to be watching her defiantly, and lifting her chin she defied them in return.

She had arranged to ride with the Earl at ten o'clock. She had in fact been ready earlier, but she thought it would be a mistake if she was downstairs waiting for him rather than that he should wait for her.

However, he was not in the Hall, but she saw him outside patting the horses and talking to the groom who was holding a very fine animal which was intended for her.

The Lyndons had never been able to afford expensive or well-bred animals, no more than a hunter for her father and another horse which her mother rode.

But Carmela had been fortunate in that she could ride the horses at the Castle, and she had been taught by the same Riding-Master as Felicity and knew that her deportment on a horse was faultless.

She thought as she came down the steps that the Earl was pleased to see her, and it might have been because she had not kept him waiting.

She expected a groom to help her into the saddle, but the Earl lifted her up, his hands at each side of her waist, saying as he did so:

"You are so light that I find it hard to believe you can handle a horse as big and spirited as Flycatcher."

"He will not bolt with me, if that is what you are afraid of," Carmela replied.

"Actually I was paying you a compliment," the Earl said drily, "and it is too early in the day to spar with anybody!"

Carmela laughed.

"I am sorry. I think actually I was afraid you might insist on my riding something docile, and I love Flycatcher!"

"Then I promise I will not take him away from you," the Earl said, and mounted his own stallion.

They galloped until there were patches of pink in Carmela's cheeks and her eyes were shining with the excitement of it.

Then as they drew in their horses to a trot and moved side by side, the Earl said:

"You ride magnificently, and I will admit again, it is something I did not expect in a girl of your age."

"I would like to point out to you," Carmela said, "that my grandmother always said the Gales never admitted to being in the wrong."

"There are exceptions to every rule."

The Earl smiled at Carmela as he replied, and they rode on for a short while without speaking.

The sun was shining, the birds were singing in the trees, the butterflies were hovering over the blossoms, and the world was so beautiful that Carmela felt at peace within herself and had no wish to fight with anybody.

Only a short while ago she had been at the Vicarage, coping with the obstructive violence of Henry and the persistent, whining complaints of Lucy.

She remembered how she had felt that the misery of it would stretch on forever into a dark future in which there was no hope.

Now, as if at the touch of a magic wand, everything was changed.

She was wearing clothes that would grace a Princess, riding a horse that was far superior to any animal she had ever seen before, and sharpening her brain beside the most attractive man she had ever met.

She ticked off her blessings one by one and told herself that she should really be on her knees saying a prayer of gratitude.

Then as she reached the last item on her list she found herself looking at the Earl and thinking that her description of him was very apt.

He was indeed most attractive when he was not being aggressive, and he was also very much a man.

Then insidiously, almost as if it intruded from a source outside her own mind, came the question:

Suppose, just suppose, she could go on riding beside him like this forever?

Chapter Five

"This morning," the Earl said as they set off from the front door, "I want to ride to the top of Gale Hill. It is something that I can remember doing when I was a boy, and being very impressed by it."

Carmela thought for a moment and vaguely remembered hearing the Countess say something about it. But it was not clear in her mind and she therefore talked of other things when they were not moving too fast for conversation.

When finally they began to climb up through the thick wood, then emerged into an area of treeless ground which rose more steeply still, she was aware that when they reached the top there should be a fine view.

They had already ridden at least three miles from the house, and the horses had to move slowly along a path that was little more than a sheep-track.

When finally they reached the top, she saw she had been right in thinking there would be a panoramic view, and there was also what looked like a stone monument.

As they dismounted she said:

"I expected a Folly. Why was that monument erected?"

"I will show you," the Earl said with a smile.

He walked ahead of her, holding his horse by the

bridle, and Carmela followed, leading Flycatcher in the same way.

Then as they reached the monument she saw that it consisted of a large flat slab with the points of the compass carved on the stone. Then the meaning of what the Countess had once said came to her and she exclaimed:

"Now I remember hearing about this!"

The Earl looked at the view in front of him, then at the compass.

There was an inscription encircling it, and Carmela read:

> *"'All the land you see from the top of this hill belongs to the Gale family, who have owned it since 1547.'"*

After she had read it aloud, the Earl said:

"I remember the first time I came here. I was so small that I found that sentence quite hard to read."

"I remember that Grandmama said it was untrue," Carmela replied, "and that on a clear day one can see into three other Counties where the land is not owned by the family."

The Earl stared at her. Then he asked:

"Is that true?"

"I am only repeating what Grandmama said to me. It was when she was reminiscing about the Estate and saying how much the Gales as a family liked to boast of their possessions."

She was teasing the Earl, and she thought he would laugh. Instead there was a scowl on his face as he looked down at the compass. Then he said violently:

"I will have that inscription removed. If there is one thing I loathe and detest, it is lies and deception of any kind!"

He was obviously so angry that Carmela looked at him in surprise, wondering why something so unimportant should affect him so tremendously.

Because the Earl went on scowling at the compass, she said:

"I am ... sorry. I did not ... mean to make you ... angry. Perhaps it would have been better if I had not repeated what Grandmama said, which may in fact not be ... true."

There was silence for a moment. Then the Earl said:

"Perhaps it is I who should apologise, but I loathe being lied to and I have just had a very unpleasant example of it."

"What has ... happened?" Carmela enquired.

For a moment she thought he would not answer and tell her what was perturbing him.

Then, almost as if he thought she had a right to know, he said:

"When I first came here I soon realised that your father had been lax in many ways, and those he employed had taken advantage of it."

"You mean they were stealing from him?" Carmela asked.

The Earl nodded.

"In quite a big way. In fact, thousands of pounds must have been lost annually, not just by petty pilfering but in well-organised theft over the whole Estate."

Carmela gave a little cry.

"How horrible! Galeston seems so perfect, which makes it doubly wrong that such things should occur beneath the beauty and peace of it."

"That is what I think," the Earl said in a hard voice, "and I have sacked the worst malefactors, although I am convinced there are others."

"What positions did they hold?" Carmela enquired.

"The worst one was the Manager, a man called Matthews," the Earl replied, "and he was aided and abetted by the Accountant, Lane, which of course made it much easier for him to operate his thefts, which have taken place over a number of years."

Carmela sighed.

"It seems to me very sad."

"It makes me very angry."

"So you dismissed them?"

"Of course," he replied. "I gave them forty-eight hours to clear out, and I told them both that as far as I was concerned they would never get employment elsewhere."

"I suppose that was what they deserved," Carmela said.

"They could have gone to prison or even been hanged or at least transported," the Earl said briefly, "but I decided to spare them because I was protecting your father's name and of course the family from the scandal of a trial."

"That was kind of you."

The Earl's lips tightened.

"My kindness was rewarded when Matthews burnt his house down before he left! I am now deciding whether I should have him arrested."

Carmela did not reply.

She was thinking that she could understand in the circumstances how bitterly he disliked lies and deception, and she was wondering what he would feel when he learnt that she had committed both offences.

She knew that it would be impossible for her to face his wrath, and that once she learnt that Felicity was married, she must run away and hide somewhere where the Earl would not find her.

Even though he had been overbearing and it was certainly wrong of him to think that he could marry her off to the Prince without any consideration for her feelings, she had no wish to hurt him.

Then she told herself that she was being presumptuous in thinking that anything she did would hurt the Earl as she would be hurt in similar circumstances.

He was so self-sufficient and so sure of himself that the only thing he would dislike would be to be proved wrong in his estimation of her.

She was aware, since they had grown more friendly and he had talked to her as if she was an equal, that he had enjoyed their conversations and their rides together almost as much as she had.

"He likes me and I think he trusts me," she told herself.

She looked down again at the compass and knew now that she dreaded the moment when the Earl would be aware that she was not what she appeared to be and had been acting a lie from the very moment of her arrival.

Because she felt embarrassed by her own thoughts and was acutely conscious of the Earl standing beside her still with the shadow of a scowl between his eyes, she forced herself to look at the view.

It stretched out towards the horizon, and below and much nearer were the house, the lake, and the gardens, looking almost like a child's model, and a very beautiful one in the sunshine.

She could see the trees in the Park, the deer moving beneath them, the swans on the lake, and the flag flying on the roof above the statues and the urns.

The Earl followed the direction of her eyes and after a moment he said quietly in a very different voice:

"I want nothing to spoil that."

"Of course not," Carmela agreed, "and I am sure that with you to look after it, it will regain its perfection and remain so."

She was speaking her thoughts aloud, then she was aware that the Earl was no longer looking at the house but at her with a faintly mocking smile on his lips.

"Are you really paying me a compliment, Felicity?" he asked. "It is something I cannot remember you doing since you first arrived here."

"You must think me very . . . remiss . . . and of course very . . . ungrateful."

"There must be a 'sting in the tail' to this conversation somewhere!" he replied.

She laughed.

"I suppose I have not been eloquent on the subject of Galeston and of you, its owner, because I have been overwhelmed by the magnificence of you both, and also because I felt . . . shy."

"And now?" the Earl enquired, raising his eyebrows.

"You are trying to force me into saying that 'familiarity breeds contempt.'"

"I was hoping," he answered, "that familiarity would make you feel friendly and happy, because that is what I want you to be."

His voice was beguiling, and she was about to say that she was happy, then she thought of why he was being so pleasant.

"If you wish me to be happy here," she said aloud, "why are you sending me away from something I am beginning to love, to a strange country which I have the feeling will never . . . really seem like . . . home?"

As she spoke she thought that her logic was unanswerable and the Earl was really being crafty in getting his own way by more subtle methods than he had used before.

To her surprise, he did not reply but merely went on staring at the house below them, although she had the feeling that he did not see it.

Then abruptly and surprisingly he said:

"I think we should start back, and we must take the horses down slowly or we might have an accident."

As he spoke she knew that he did not want to go on talking to her, and she thought perhaps he was nervous of her using the Prince's absence as an opportunity to make him change his mind about their marriage.

Because she had no wish to annoy him, she replied:

"Perhaps you would be kind enough to help me mount Flycatcher. I do not think I can manage alone."

"Yes, of course," the Earl agreed.

He slipped his horse's bridle over his arm and lifted her skilfully onto the saddle, then arranged her skirt over the stirrup.

"Thank you," Carmela said.

She was looking down at him and as she spoke he raised his head and looked up at her.

Their eyes met and she had a sudden strange feeling that he was saying something to her that he had not said before and that it was important.

But then the Earl looked away and busied himself mounting his own horse, and she thought she must have been mistaken.

Nevertheless, as she started down the hill she had the strange feeling that her heart was beating unaccountably fast.

They rode back through the wood, then returned towards the house, taking a different route back.

It was nearly noon when finally they rode through the Park and trotted towards the bridge which spanned the lake.

As soon as the front of the house came in sight they became aware of three carriages drawn up outside the front door.

Carmela gave a little gasp.

"You did not tell me you had friends coming to luncheon!"

"I invited nobody," the Earl answered briefly.

"Then who is here?"

"I may be wrong," he replied, "but I have a feeling you are going to meet a number of our relatives."

"Oh, no, I hope not!" Carmela exclaimed in dismay, but the Earl was right.

* * *

Afterwards, Carmela thought she might have expected that sooner or later the "grapevine," or the gossip which in the country was carried on the wind, would bring the Gale relatives flocking to the big house to make the acquaintance of the girl they supposed was Felicity.

As soon as Carmela had changed from her riding-habit into a pretty gown, she entered the Salon and saw by their resemblance to the portraits on the walls that the people gathered there were undoubtedly Gales.

A few of the women were attractive, though certainly they were not as pretty as Felicity. At the same time, most of them bore a vague resemblance to one another and they were on the whole a surprisingly good-looking family.

What was really surprising was that they had called not only because they had learnt that she was a guest in the house but because they also knew that the Countess had left her a huge fortune.

A short while after she had been introduced to each member of the family one by one, she learnt the truth of this from an elderly relative who drew her to a sofa and said:

"I have always been anxious to meet you again, Felicity, although I doubt if you will remember how often I used to see you as a child."

"I am afraid . . . not."

"You had great difficulty in pronouncing my name, which is Cousin Louise," the relative went on. "I was devoted to your grandmother, and hardly a week went by when we did not meet and gossip together."

"You must have missed her when she left," Carmela replied.

"I not only missed her but I was deeply hurt that she did not reply to the letters I wrote to her."

Carmela felt there was nothing she could say to this and therefore she remained silent.

"When I learnt that she had died and had not even left me a memento of what I believed was a deep affection we had for each other, I could hardly believe it!"

"I do not think Grandmama left mementoes to anybody," Carmela said consolingly.

"I know that!" came the response. "You have had everything! You must consider yourself very lucky to have such a fortune when all the rest of the family has been ignored and neglected."

Because the voice was now sharp, Carmela wondered how she had learnt of the Countess's Will, since Felicity and the Earl had said it was a secret.

"When I went to the Office of the family Solicitors," the cousin went on, "and demanded to hear the contents of your grandmother's Will, I could hardly believe my ears when he told me how wealthy she had become in the years after she left here."

Carmela thought it extremely pushy of the relative to have made such demands, and she wondered why the Solicitor had been so indiscreet.

Then, as if the Earl sensed her discomfiture, he came to her side to say:

"I think, Felicity, you must not allow the Duchess to monopolise you when your other relatives are longing to talk to you."

Carmela immediately rose to her feet, but the Earl had answered her question, and she now knew that the family Solicitor had been too over-awed by the Duchess to refuse to give her the information.

The other cousins were not quite so distinguished.

A number of the ladies had married important noblemen in the neighbourhood, although it was difficult for Carmela to understand who they were or where they fitted into Felicity's family-tree.

She was also to find that having arrived uninvited to call on the head of the family, they all expected to stay to luncheon and were quite surprised when he asked them if that was their intention.

"Of course, Selwyn!" she heard one Dowager say. "You can hardly expect us to make the journey home without first having some refreshment!"

They had all by this time been provided with champagne, and Carmela thought it quite a remarkable feat on the part of the Chef when only twenty minutes later than usual they sat down to an excellent meal which might have been planned several days previously.

The conversation she had had with the Duchess had made her realise that her supposed relatives were looking at her not only with curiosity but with envy and undoubtedly a certain amount of malice.

She could hear the sharpness in their voices when they asked her what were her plans for the future and where she intended to live.

"She can come to me if she wishes," the Duchess said on hearing this question.

Before Carmela could answer, someone said:

"You know you would find that an inconvenience, Louise. I was in fact thinking that Felicity would fit in very well with my household. After all, Mary is nearly the same age as she is, and the two girls could do things together."

This statement evoked a storm of argument, and soon it seemed to Carmela that they were all fighting over her as if she were a bone amongst a lot of hungry dogs.

She knew that all this concern was due entirely to Felicity's enormous fortune.

She could not help feeling what a bomb-shell it would be if she suddenly announced that she was quite penniless and would be delighted to have a comfortable home to go to when she was no longer at Galeston.

She was quite certain that there would be a sudden silence and the offers of hospitality would die away on the lips of those who had made them.

If anything was needed to convince her that Felicity had been right in running away with Jimmy, it was this.

She suddenly felt ashamed that people who were so well born and comparatively wealthy in their own right should sink to grubbing for more and in doing so reveal their greed so obviously.

There came an end to this discussion only when the Earl said, speaking in his most autocratic voice:

"I am sure you are all very generous in offering Felicity a home, but as her Guardian I have made quite extensive plans for her future and you will be informed of them in due course."

"Plans?" the Duchess exclaimed. "But why, Selwyn, should you concern yourself with Felicity?"

"Because Felicity is an orphan and I am head of the family!" the Earl said curtly.

There was silence while obviously the Gales could think of no answer to this. Because they looked so discomfitted, Carmela said in her quiet, sweet voice:

"Thank you . . . very much all the same for being so . . . kind. I am very . . . touched that you should want me, and now I do not feel so alone as I did . . . before."

"Oh, you sweet child, you need never feel alone!" one of the relatives exclaimed. "After all, we are all Gales and we must help one another and stick together."

"Of course," the Duchess said. "Did any of us even think of doing anything else?"

The unspoken answer was that it was the Countess who had cut herself off from them all and in doing so had taken Felicity away from them too.

But as this was something they had no wish to declare openly, there was a pause, and then the conversation started on a different subject and for the moment Felicity's future was forgotten.

It was only after luncheon when they were all leaving that one by one they drew Carmela aside, out of ear-shot of the others, to say:

"We have no wish to upset Selwyn's plans for you, dear child, but do let *me* know if you are not happy."

The Duchess, however, put it more bluntly.

"If you are being pushed into doing anything you do not wish to do," she said sharply, "I will look after you, if only for your father's sake."

"Thank you," Carmela said.

The Duchess then took her by the arm and drew her a little to one side.

"Now listen, child," she said. "Do not be in a hurry to get married to the first man who asks you. With a fortune like yours, you can pick and choose."

Carmela smiled but said nothing.

"And it would be commonsense," the Duchess continued, "to ask my advice before you accept anyone."

"It is very kind of you to worry about me, Ma'am."

There was a pause, then the Duchess said:

"I hear there was a foreign Prince staying here. Is he a suitor for your hand?"

There seemed to be no reason why she should not tell the truth, and Carmela answered quietly:

"I think so."

The Duchess snorted.

"I might have guessed that when I learnt this morning that he had been here. You be careful of foreigners. They cannot be trusted, and when it comes to husbands there is no-one like an Englishman. You take my word for it."

"I will remember what you said, Ma'am," Carmela replied.

The Duchess glanced down the room to where the Earl was talking to another relative.

"Selwyn has been abroad for a long time," she said as if she was speaking to herself. "He will settle down to our ways in a year or so—at least, that is what we can all hope."

The way the Duchess spoke seemed to Carmela so amusing that she almost laughed aloud.

Fortunately, before she could make any response, another relative interrupted them to say to Carmela:

"I live only four miles away, and I suggest, Felicity, that you come to luncheon with us next Sunday. I am very, very anxious for you to meet my two sons. They are both of them, although I say it, very charming, and it is a good thing for cousins to become friendly with each other."

"What you are hoping," the Duchess interposed tartly, "is that Felicity will marry one of them. If she does, she will need all her money to maintain them at the gaming-tables!"

"How can you say anything so unkind, Louise?" the affronted mother asked in plaintive tones.

"I always speak the truth, you know that," the Duchess replied, "and that is why Felicity should listen to me and not to all the 'soft soap' the rest of you are handing her. I am going now."

The Duchess walked away to say good-bye to the Earl, and the mother of the two sons said to Carmela:

"Do not listen to Cousin Louise. Although we all respect her, she is an embittered woman in many ways. Promise me you will accept my invitation."

"I will discuss it with His Lordship," Carmela replied. "As you realise, I shall have to have his permission."

"Yes, of course," was the answer. "At the same time, although Selwyn obviously takes his duties as head of the family very seriously, he is really too young to be an entirely suitable Guardian for a young girl."

"I think that is something I must decide for myself," the Earl interposed.

Both Carmela and the lady to whom she was speaking started, not having heard him approach.

"I have no wish to offend you!" the lady with the sons exclaimed quickly. "I was just thinking that dear Felicity might be happier in a family."

The Earl did not reply, but Carmela, seeing a twinkle in his eyes, realised that he was as amused as she was at the offers of hospitality that Felicity's fortune, rather than Felicity herself, was evoking.

When finally the last Gale relative had said her farewells, the Earl exclaimed:

"I hope you enjoyed that exhibition of blatant hypocrisy!"

Carmela laughed.

"I wonder," he went on, "if they would have pressed many invitations on you if you were penniless."

It was what Carmela had thought herself, but she replied:

"Perhaps they were really meaning to be kind."

"People are always kind to the rich."

"I think that is a very cynical remark!" Carmela said provocatively. "It may be true of some people, but not all."

"Where your relatives are concerned, I should take everything they say to you with a good 'pinch of salt'!"

"That might well include you," she answered.

"I might have guessed you would make that comment," he replied, "and when I suggested you should marry Prince Frederich, I was genuinely convinced that from a woman's point of view nothing could be more advantageous or more attractive."

He spoke with an unmistakable sincerity and Carmela knew that it was the truth.

However, to tease him she said:

"Well, at least now I have quite a considerable choice! I realise that all my relatives have at the back of their minds some aspirant for my hand . . . and of course for my pocket!"

"Who is being cynical now?" the Earl asked. "And anyway, may I point out that you have to obtain my approval before you can marry anybody?"

"Are you saying that you might bar your own kith and kin from the competition?" Carmela asked. "I have a feeling they would consider that most unsporting, as you yourself have your money on another horse."

The Earl laughed and it was a sound of genuine amusement.

"You continue to surprise me, Felicity," he said. "I am sure most women would not look upon their marriage in such a frivolous manner."

"Would you prefer me to squint down my nose and look coy?" Carmela asked. "I certainly felt like that when my marriage was first mentioned, but now it

seems to be a general topic of conversation and I find it
hard to blush."

The Earl was silent for a moment. Then he said:

"I have the impression, Felicity, that you are not
taking this subject, which should be an absorbing one
for you, as seriously as I would wish."

He paused for a moment before he went on:

"I cannot explain quite what I mean. As I have said
before, I am very ignorant where young girls are concerned, but there is something—I cannot put my finger
on it, but it is nevertheless there—which tells me that
you are playing with me."

Carmela thought he was more perceptive than she
had expected.

Although he was finding it hard to put into words,
some instinct was telling him that she was not really
frightened of being swept up the aisle as the bride of
the Prince and that, in a way which he could not
determine, she would ultimately elude him.

She thought it was doubtless the first time he had
been really puzzled by somebody who came under his
command.

She knew too that it was his long experience of
leadership when dealing with all sorts and conditions of
people which told him that she was not exactly what
she appeared to be, although he could find no logical
explanation for it.

Because she thought it was a mistake to let him
dwell too long on this aspect of her behaviour, she said:

"I refuse to worry about it just now, and if you
remember, we had arranged this afternoon to see if we
could catch any fish in the lake as you used to do when
you were a boy."

"I had not forgotten, but I thought you had," the
Earl replied.

"Now you are fishing in a different sort of way,"
Carmela said with a smile, "and what are we waiting
for?"

The Earl laughed and they walked through the

front door and across the lawn in the direction of the lake.

* * *

When Carmela went to bed that night, she thought she had never enjoyed an evening more.

To be able to talk to the Earl alone, without his continually deferring politely to the Prince, and to argue with him over a dozen different subjects was an enchantment that she could hardly put into words.

It had left her with a feeling of happiness that she had not known since her father had died. They had often sat at the Dining-Room table for hours after their small meal was finished, simply because it was easier to talk with what her father called "their elbows on the table" than to move to the Sitting-Room.

But while their bodies were stationary their minds had flown out over the whole Universe, covering many countries, peoples, religions, and philosophies. For Carmela it had meant finding new horizons or, as her father had sometimes said, exploring "the mountains of the mind," of which she had not previously been aware.

She felt the same when talking with the Earl, and when at last they walked together towards the Salon he said:

"How can you be so intelligent when I expected you to be very different?"

"Gauche and nit-witted, I think, was the right description," Carmela said with a smile.

"I know now that I have not only to reassess you but to polish up my own knowledge and intelligence," the Earl said.

"That is certainly a confession, which I wish I could press like a flower and put in a scrap-book," Carmela teased.

They laughed, then talked seriously until finally and reluctantly Carmela felt that she should go to bed.

"You did suggest riding early tomorrow?" she asked.

"I thought we might go to the far end of the Estate," he said, "and as it will take several hours, if you could face bread and cheese at a wayside Inn, we could make an expedition of it."

"I would love that, and I like bread and cheese."

"Very well," the Earl replied. "That is what we will do, and I will order breakfast for eight o'clock, if you can be down by then."

"I shall not be late," Carmela promised. "Goodnight, Cousin Selwyn, I have enjoyed this evening."

"So have I," the Earl admitted.

She curtseyed to him, and to her surprise he took her hand in his.

"Good-night, Felicity," he said. "Please continue to surprise and perhaps I should say dazzle me, as it is something I enjoy."

He spoke quite seriously, then he lifted her hand to his lips and kissed it.

It was not what Carmela had expected, and as she felt the pressure of his mouth on her skin it gave her a strange sensation she had never known before.

For a moment she was still, looking at the Earl a little questioningly.

Then because she was shy, she took away her hand and leaving the Salon hurried across the Hall and up the stairs without looking back.

She had the feeling that he was watching her, but she told herself she was probably imagining it.

In her bedroom an elderly housemaid helped her to undress, and when she got into bed she lay thinking of the Earl and of the way he had kissed her hand.

It was what she might have expected the Prince to do, but not the Earl. Yet, it had seemed to come quite naturally to him, and she knew that because he was so athletic he had a grace which made him never appear clumsy or ungainly in any way.

She looked back over the things they had said to each other and thought they might almost have been

taking part in one of the witty Restoration Plays that she
had sometimes read aloud to her father in the evenings.

'I suppose that because he has such a sharp brain
and is so intelligent, he makes me intelligent too,' she
thought.

She began to think of things she could say to him
the next day that would sound witty or provocative.

She had almost fallen asleep when she heard her
bedroom door open.

Then there was a light in the room and she realised
it came from a candle held in somebody's hand.

"Wh-what . . . is it?" she asked.

As a figure approached her bed she saw that it was
one of the younger maids who sometimes helped the
elderly housemaid who usually looked after her.

"What is it, Suzy?" she asked again.

"I'm sorry to wake you, M'Lady," Suzy replied,
"but His Lordship asks if you'll go downstairs. There's
been an accident and he wants your help."

"An accident?" Carmela exclaimed as she sat up in
bed. "What sort of an accident?"

"I thinks it's one o' the dogs, M'Lady. His Lordship said as I were to fetch you."

Carmela got out of bed.

As she did so, she thought that there were several
dogs that were kept in the stables and because they
were not trained they were not allowed into the house.

"I want dogs of my own which will always be with
me," the Earl had told her, "but I thought there were
too many other things for me to do first before I could
take on any others."

However, she had noticed that whenever he went
to the stables he patted the dogs that were kept there
in the kennels, and they would jump up and make a
fuss over him.

She thought one of these must have been hurt in
some way, and as she slipped on a pair of soft slippers
she looked round for a dressing-gown.

The one she had been wearing was of very thin material trimmed with lace, but Suzy went to the wardrobe and brought out one of heavy satin with an inter-lining, which was really a winter garment and too warm for the spring.

Carmela thought as Suzy helped her into it that it was certainly more modest than anything lighter.

As she fastened the little pearl buttons that went all the way down the front, she thought that enveloping though it was, some of the Gale relatives who had called today would be shocked at her going downstairs in her night-attire.

However, she was not concerned with their feelings but only with the fact that the Earl needed her.

"Has His Lordship got bandages?" she asked.

"Yes, M'Lady," the maid replied. "He's everything like that, but he wants your help."

Carmela brushed her hair back quickly from her forehead and said:

"I am ready!"

"I'll lead the way, M'Lady."

Picking up the candle, Suzy went out the door and into the passage.

She shut the door behind her, then set off quickly along the corridor which led towards the top of the Grand Staircase, but she did not descend it.

Instead, she walked on towards the West Wing of the house until they came to a narrow staircase down which Suzy hurried.

In fact, she moved so quickly that they were now away from the light of candles in the main part of the building, and Carmela was afraid of being left behind in the dark.

They reached an unlit passage which she thought must be near the servants' part of the house, but Suzy went on and still on without looking back.

Carmela thought they were going in the direction of the stables and that was where the Earl must be with the injured dog. Then suddenly Suzy stopped and took a side-passage which led, Carmela could see, to an outer door.

Now she was eager to reach the Earl and find out exactly what was happening.

Suzy opened the door, which was unlocked, and walked outside into the darkness. Carmela followed her, then as she stepped out into the night, suddenly something thick, dark, and enveloping was thrown over her head.

She gave a cry of terror, but even as she did so she realised that her voice was stifled by the thickness of the covering.

At the same time, rough arms picked her up.

"What is . . . happening? Put me . . . down!" she tried to say.

But her voice lost, and the arms which were encircling her held her so tightly that she felt as if the breath was squeezed out of her body.

Then roughly she was dumped inside what she realised was a carriage, because almost before she was seated, horses started to move and she could feel wheels revolving under her.

Then as the terror of what was happening swept over her, she knew she was being kidnapped!

Chapter Six

The carriage was bumping very awkwardly over rough ground, perhaps even grass without a track, and she wondered frantically where she was being taken and who was beside her.

Even through the thickness of the cloth which covered her down to her knees, she was uncomfortably aware of a man sitting there.

He had taken his arms from her once he had thrown her down in the carriage, but the mere fact that he was close was frightening to the point where all she wanted to do was scream.

However, she realised that this was hopeless, first because she was sensible enough to know that nobody else would hear her, and secondly because it was difficult even to breathe through the thickness of the material in which she was enveloped.

She imagined it was some kind of felt, because while it was pliable and seemed to cling to her face, it was unpleasantly rough.

She was not much worried about the discomfort but only about what was going to happen to her and why she was being kidnapped.

The motive for this, however, was not too difficult to determine.

Now that the extent of Felicity's fortune was known to all the Gales, it would also have been gossipped about in the country, and both the gentlefolk and their servants would be aware of it.

It seemed obvious that somebody was going to hold her for ransom, and she only hoped that the Earl would pay up without any delay.

Then she remembered that if he did so it would be impossible for her to repay him unless Felicity gave her the money.

The fact that she was absolutely penniless made everything more complicated, and she wondered what Felicity would have done in the circumstances if it was she who had been abducted as her captors intended.

'The one thing I must not do,' Carmela thought to herself, 'is to defy them in any way.'

She had read stories of people being tortured because they would not reveal where some treasure or their money was hidden, and she knew that she was a coward!

She thought that if she was threatened, she would be far too afraid to do anything but agree to what was demanded.

At the same time, it struck her that the Earl might have very different ideas.

She knew that nothing would infuriate him more than finding himself in the ignominious position of having to pay a ransom for her without being able to arrest the criminals who asked for it.

'Suppose he refuses to pay?' she thought frantically.

She felt herself shiver with fear lest those demanding the ransom might in that case punish her for his obstinacy.

She remembered stories of how in the East a victim in the same circumstances as herself could be mutilated in order to exact the payment of the price demanded.

First would be sent a finger, then an ear, and finally a nose to those who were refusing to pay the ransom.

The idea was so horrifying that Carmela wished she were unconscious so that she would not think of such things, but she knew that instinctively she would strive to the utmost to keep herself alive and to retain her ability to think.

On and on the carriage travelled.

Although she could move her hands underneath the heavy cloth, she was afraid to pull it up in case the man sitting next to her might stop her by force.

Suddenly she became aware that one of her feet was very cold and she realised that she had lost a slipper when being carried from the doorstep of the house into the carriage.

She rubbed her foot against her ankle very slowly and gently so as not to draw attention to herself, and then as she listened intently she thought she could hear the man breathing heavily.

He coughed once and moved restlessly, and with the sway of the carriage his shoulder knocked against hers and she cringed away from him as far as she could into the corner.

Now the horses were moving very slowly and she thought the ground beneath the wheels was rougher than ever.

She knew they had travelled quite a long way from the house, and she thought despairingly that even if the Earl searched for her thoroughly, he might never be able to find her.

The horses came to a halt, the man beside her opened the carriage door, and for the first time she heard his voice.

"Can't you get any nearer, Arthur?"

It was not an educated voice, but it was certainly not as coarse as she had anticipated.

Then she heard another man answer:

"No, we'd get stuck in the trees."

"All right then," the first man said. "Tie up the horses and bring the lantern."

The word "trees" told Carmela that they must be in a wood of some sort.

The man got out of the carriage on his side, there was a pause, then he opened the door on her side and pulled her into his arms.

Again she wanted to scream but somehow prevented herself from doing so.

The man was obviously large and strong, for it seemed no effort for him to carry her with one arm round her body and the other under her knees.

Now she could hear dry twigs cracking under his feet and she was aware that he was not walking along a straight path but twisting, she presumed, between tree-trunks.

They walked for some way, then stopped.

"Open the door," he said.

"Mind your head," the other man warned.

He walked on a few steps more, and then Carmela was set down on a hard floor.

Now she steadied herself with her hands, and she found that she was touching not boards but ordinary earth which was dry and hard as if it had been trodden down.

She could hear the two men who had brought her there moving about, and fearing they might trip over her feet and hurt the one which was bare, she pulled them close to her body.

Then suddenly and so unexpectedly that it gave her a shock, the cloth that covered her was pulled away and she could see.

The first thing she was aware of was two men's faces staring at her in the light of a lantern.

One man was middle-aged. He was not as rough as Carmela had expected and was obviously not a labourer, and he had an intelligent face.

The other man was younger, thin and pale with a long nose, and was wearing spectacles.

Neither of them spoke, and Carmela drew in her breath and asked:

"Who . . . are you . . . and why have you . . . brought me . . . here?"

As she spoke she thought it was a foolish question.

At the same time, she was pleased that her voice did not tremble, although because she was breathless it was not very loud.

The older man smiled unpleasantly.

"I'll tell you why we've brought you here, Lady Felicity," he said. "We want money, and we want it quickly!"

"I doubt if His Lordship . . . my Guardian, will . . . give it to . . . you," Carmela replied.

The man laughed.

"You don't suppose we're going to ask him for it?"

He looked at the man with the glasses and said:

"Come on, Arthur, you tell her what she's got to do."

It was then that Carmela realised that the other man was standing by a large, roughly made wooden box and was taking some papers from his pocket to place them beside the lantern.

"All you've got to do, M'Lady," he said in a slightly high-pitched voice, "is to sign this cheque I've made out for you and also a letter I've written on your behalf."

Carmela did not speak and after a moment the other man said:

"We're only asking for our rights and what we're entitled to."

"What do you mean by that?" Carmela asked, since he seemed to expect her to reply.

"Your Guardian, as you call him, has after years of hard work thrown me out without a penny, and Lane here's in the same position."

It was then that Carmela knew who these men were.

They were the Manager and the Accountant who had made the Earl so angry because they had robbed the Estate, and it was Matthews who had burnt his house down before leaving.

It flashed through her mind that she should confront them by saying they were fortunate not to have been imprisoned or hanged.

Then she knew it would be a foolish thing to do and nothing she could say would change their intention of extracting money from her.

She also knew that if she told them she did not actually own any money, they would only laugh and not believe her.

They seemed to be waiting for her to say something, and after a moment she said:

"When I have signed the cheque as you have . . . asked me to do . . . what do you intend to . . . do with me?"

There was a tremor in her voice in the last three words, and she lifted her chin higher as if to refute it.

Matthews smiled again, unpleasantly.

"I expect you'll be found sooner or later," he said, "and if you feel a bit hungry while you're waiting, you can always remember that that's what your nice, kind Guardian intended us to be."

"You realise that if you are caught obtaining money by . . . blackmail," Carmela said, "it will be added to your other crimes and the . . . penalties will be very . . . severe?"

"We won't be caught," Matthews replied. "We're going abroad, aren't we, Arthur? But you might ask His Lordship, if he's feeling generous, to look after our families for us."

He smirked before he added:

"There'll be plenty of women where we're going!"

"You are talking too much," Lane said. "Come on, let's get on with it."

As he spoke, Carmela was sure that Matthews had been drinking, perhaps to give himself "Dutch Courage."

As he moved to pull her to her feet, she could smell the drink on his breath and knew she was right.

Loathing the touch of his hand on her arm, she shook herself free of him and tried to walk with dignity to the wooden box, but she found it difficult with only one shoe, and the ground hurt her bare foot.

Then as she reached the box she saw there was a block of wood behind it to be used as a seat.

As Carmela seated herself, Lane took from a small leather bag an ink-well which he opened and two quill-pens.

He put them in front of her and she saw that the letter he had written was in the flowing script of a clerk.

She picked it up and read it.

> *To Messrs. Coutts:*
> *Sirs, Will you kindly cash the enclosed cheque*
> *for the sum of ten thousand pounds made*
> *payable to F. J. Matthews.*
>
> *Yours truly,*

Carmela looked at the top of the letter and saw that it was embossed with the Earl's coronet over the words "Galeston Park," and knew that Lane had stolen it before he left.

The two men were watching her as she put down the letter and said:

"And you really think that the Bank will hand over such a large sum without making further enquiries?"

"Why not?" Lane asked. "Your life's worth a great deal more, Your Ladyship, but we're being sensible and asking for a sum that'll not make them suspicious."

"If you ask me," Matthews said before Carmela

could speak, "we should demand a great deal more. Make it twenty thousand pounds, Arthur. We can do with it."

Lane shook his head.

"No! They would think it strange that the young lady would want so much in cash. They may think that anyway."

"You told me ten thousand was safe!" Matthews argued aggressively.

"Nothing's safe," Lane answered. "But I thought, seeing how wealthy Her Ladyship is, they'll think she's buying horses or jewellery and will not query the letter or the cheque."

"If you're wrong, I'll murder you!" Matthews said. "Well, get on with it!"

Lane looked towards Carmela and pointed with his finger to the bottom of the page.

"Sign your name here, M'Lady."

Carmela was debating whether she should sign the letter in a passable imitation of Felicity's writing, or make it so different that the Bank would instantly be suspicious and refuse to give the two men any money.

For a moment she thought this was a brilliant idea and they would get the punishment they richly deserved.

Then she thought that on the first sign of hesitation by the Bank they would run away, and it might be some time before Coutts could get in touch with her to tell her what had occurred.

All that time she would be imprisoned here in the wooden hut which she supposed had been erected by wood-cutters.

If the Earl did not find her in the meantime, she could be a prisoner for days or weeks with no chance of escape.

She thought that in act her only chance for freedom would be to bargain with the men who were threatening her.

She did not pick up the pen but merely said:

"If I sign this and you receive the money, will you then come back and set me free?"

Matthews hesitated, and she knew his instinct was to say that she could rot here for all he cared.

Then a crafty look came into his eyes as he replied:

"Of course, M'Lady! That'd be only fair, wouldn't it, as you're being fair to us?"

He was lying, and Carmela knew he had no intention of returning to release her. The moment they had the money, he and Lane would go abroad.

'I will sign Felicity's name in my own writing,' she decided.

Then as if he read her thoughts Lane said:

"If you try to trick us, M'Lady, you'll be sorry!"

"What do you mean, trick us?" Matthews asked. "What're you thinking she might do?"

"She could sign in such a way that the Bank wouldn't honour the cheque," Lane replied, "and that's what I suspect she's thinking of doing."

Matthews gave a snarl of rage that was like that of a wild animal.

"You dare!" he said to Carmela. "If you do anything like that, I'll bash your face in! I've had enough from His Lordship without any more from you!"

Carmela felt as if her heart contracted in fear, and she said hesitatingly:

"I . . . I will sign it as you . . . want me to do."

"You'd better!" Matthews said menacingly.

He turned to Lane to ask:

"Do you know what her signature looks like?"

"How should I know?"

"Then we'll have to trust her."

"I agree," Lane said, "and you've promised her that once we have the money we'll come back and set her free."

He spoke with a note in his voice which was intended to warn Matthews that that was the one way they could be certain she would sign as they wanted, but Matthews, stupid with drink, did not understand.

"I'm not coming back to this da . . ."

He realised as he was about to swear that Lane was making a signal to him behind Carmela's back, and with difficulty he prevented the words from leaving his lips.

"All right," he said. "Have it your own way. "We'll come back."

Carmela thought with a little sigh that it was hopeless.

They had no intention of returning, but she was too afraid to trick them in case they avenged themselves on her physically.

Without saying anything more, she dipped the quill-pen into the ink-well, and then slowly, because she had to be careful how she forged Felicity's name, she signed the letter.

Then Lane produced the cheque for her.

It had been printed for another Bank and he had carefully crossed out the name of it and instead had written under it: *"Coutts and Company."*

As Carmela looked at it she thought how much ten thousand pounds would have meant to her father and mother and how they had often to pinch and scrape along on a few pounds a month when her father was unable to sell one of his pictures.

Then she told herself that although it seemed an enormous sum to her, Felicity's fortune was so large that if Matthews and Lane did get away with it, the loss would not matter greatly.

She therefore signed Felicity's name without saying anything further, and as she did so, both Matthews and Lane were watching every movement of the pen.

Then as Lane sanded the cheque, Matthews said:

"Now then, let's see how quickly those horses you've hired can get us to London."

"We'll be there before the Bank opens," Lane replied.

He put the cheque and the letter in his pocket,

screwed down the ink-well, and put it and the pens
back into the bag.

"I hope you'll be comfortable, M'Lady," Matthews
said mockingly. "And while you're here you can medi-
tate on the old adage: 'He laughs longer who laughs
last.'"

As he spoke he walked towards the door and bent
his head to pass through it, and was followed by Lane
carrying the lantern.

"Please, do not leave me here in the dark!" Carmela
cried.

But by this time they were outside the hut, and
the only answer was a creak of the door as they pressed
it into place.

Then she heard the bolt slammed down and knew
she was a prisoner, for the door could not be opened
except from the outside.

She was now in complete darkness, and she knew
there was no window in the hut, since otherwise she
would have seen the light from the lantern as they
walked away through the trees.

She was still sitting on the rough piece of wood
that she had used as a seat, and the box was in front of
her.

She put her hands together and tried to think how
long it would be before there was any chance of her
being rescued.

Now she was aware that she was shivering not only
from fear but from cold, and the foot without a shoe was
beginning to feel numb.

"I must be sensible," Carmela told herself, "and
wait until it is daylight, then I shall have some idea if
there is any means by which I can escape."

However, she had the feeling that it was going to
be impossible.

She had seen the huts that the wood-cutters made
in which to keep their tools and where they sat when
the weather was too wet for work.

She knew they were usually constructed of tree-trunks split down the middle and hammered deep into the ground. The roof would be made in the same way and covered with something to make it rain-proof.

Because tools were valuable, no wood-cutter would wish to lose his saw or his axe, and therefore the huts were usually solidly constructed and impervious to thieves.

'Perhaps I shall never be found,' Carmela thought dismally. 'I will die of starvation and all that will remain will be my bones.'

Then she told herself that it was wrong to think of anything so depressing.

She had to believe that God would look after her and that He would hear her prayers.

Being really rather frightened, she thought she would be wise to sit down on the ground with her back against the wall and perhaps in a little while she would be able to sleep.

She groped her way along the side of the hut and sat down in a corner, covering her feet as best she could with her dressing-gown.

As she touched it she thought she should be grateful to Suzy for having chosen something so warm, then she knew as she thought about it that Suzy was obviously in league with Matthews and Lane.

'How angry that will make the Earl,' she thought, 'that another of his staff has deceived him! And Suzy is a servant in the house.'

She could almost feel sorry for him, until she remembered that she too was lying, she too was deceiving him.

Yet, she felt sure that when he learnt that she was missing he would use all his perception and all his determination to find her and bring her back.

The earliest time he could know about it would be when she was not there to breakfast with him at eight o'clock in the morning, as they had planned.

Then he would know that something was wrong.

He would hardly believe that she had run away when she had taken no clothes from the house except for her dressing-gown. The elderly maid would be able to inform him of that.

'He will find me... I know he will... find me!' Carmela thought.

She knew it would be a long time until he did so, but she felt as if the idea lifted her heart like a light in the darkness.

She leant back against the wall and listened, and now in the silence of the hut she could hear faintly the sounds of the wood outside.

Far away in the distance there was the bark of a fox, and an owl hooted overhead, and although she could not be certain, she thought there was the scamper of tiny feet.

She knew that if she were outside she would not be afraid.

The wood was very much a part of the fairy-stories her father had told her when she was a child.

Now she wished that the goblins that burrowed under the trees would come up through the floor of the hut to help her, or perhaps the birds would carry a message to the Earl to wake him and tell him of the danger she was in.

Because she could not send a bird, she felt as if instead she sent her thoughts winging their way across the trees towards the great house.

"Help me! Help me!" she called.

But she thought that although the Earl might be perceptive in some ways, they were not so closely attuned to each other that he would understand her need.

Then she remembered the way he had kissed her hand when they had said good-night to each other, and she thought she could still feel his lips warm and somehow possessive on her skin.

"Help me! Help me!"

She felt again as if her vibrations flew like birds from her prison towards the only person who could save her.

Then as her whole mind and body yearned for him, she knew as if forked lightning flashed through her that she loved him.

* * *

The Earl awoke with a feeling of satisfaction because something enjoyable lay ahead.

He remembered the plans he had made with Felicity for an expedition on horse-back, and he thought it was something he would enjoy enormously, besides bringing him a new knowledge of his Estate.

He stretched out his arms as he yawned, then he remembered that he had woken in the night, feeling that something was perturbing him, although he could not think what it could be.

He had in fact lain awake for some time and found himself thinking of how attractive and how unexpectedly intelligent Felicity was.

'She could never bore me,' he thought, 'but brains are wasted on a woman.'

He knew that when he had a son he would want him to be clever as well as athletic, but he had never thought that necessary for any daughters he might have.

Now he told himself that while it might be a dangerous precedent for a woman to have a brain, it certainly made her more interesting to her husband.

'The Prince will not be bored very quickly with Felicity,' he thought.

Then wondered if the Prince's brain would equal hers.

"I expect what will happen soon or later is that she will rule Horngelstein," he told himself, "and there will be nothing Frederich can do to prevent it."

He thought that he himself would dislike a woman who bossed him because she was cleverer than he was.

Then he told himself that when he found this mythical wife to give him the children he needed to carry on the inheritance from father to son, she might as well be clever rather than stupid.

He remembered all the women with whom he had had tempestuous but short affairs, but he could not remember one who had talked to him on serious subjects or had stimulated his brain as Felicity had managed to do.

He knew that today when they stopped for luncheon at some country Inn she would amuse and tease him.

He enjoyed it when she looked at him from under her eye-lashes, which curled back like a child's. There would be a mischievous sparkle in her eyes which he had grown to recognise.

"Dammit all!" he told himself. "She is far too good for young Frederich! He will just be enamoured of her because she has a pretty face and will not appreciate the twists and turns of her exceptional brain."

As he thought about Felicity she seemed very vivid in his mind, in fact so vivid that she might have been standing beside the bed talking to him.

Then he turned over and forced himself to think of other things so that he could go to sleep again.

＊　　＊　　＊

The Earl's valet came softly into the room to set down beside the bed a tray on which there was a pot of tea and a wafer-thin slice of bread and butter.

He then crossed to the windows to pull back the curtains and let in the morning sunshine.

"It is a nice day, Jarvis," the Earl remarked.

"Yes, M'Lord. Excuse me, M'Lord, but Mrs. Humphries is worried."

"Worried? What has she to be worried about?"

The Earl poured some tea into the cup as he spoke.

"She can't find Her Ladyship, M'Lord!"

The Earl looked surprised.

"What do you mean—she cannot find Her Lady-ship?"

"Well, M'Lord, she's not in her room. She asked to be woken early so as to go riding with Your Lordship, but she doesn't appear to be anywhere else."

"She must have got up early and gone to the stables," the Earl suggested.

"No, M'Lord. Mrs. Humphries has already thought of that, and Her Ladyship's not dressed. In fact, the only thing missing from her wardrobe, Mrs. Humphries says, is a thick dressing-down Her Ladyship hasn't worn since she has been here."

"It certainly sounds a mystery," the Earl said good-humouredly, "but I expect there is a simple explana-tion."

As he spoke he thought that perhaps Felicity had gone up to the roof to see the dawn rising or into the Library to choose some particular book she wanted to read.

He always thought Mrs. Humphries was an old "fuss-pot," and this was a very good example of it.

There was a knock on the door and Jarvis went to open it.

He spoke to somebody outside and a minute later came back into the room.

"What is it?" the Earl asked, sipping his tea.

"Mrs. Humphries asked me to tell you, M'Lord, that one of the lower housemaids just found this outside the door that leads to the back driveway."

As Jarvis spoke he held out to the Earl a pale mauve satin slipper.

"You say this was found on the back drive?" the Earl asked.

"Yes, M'Lord, and Mr. Newman says there's signs of carriage wheels which he would swear weren't there yesterday evening when he came in that way."

The Earl put down his cup and got quickly out of bed.

He dressed hurriedly and went from his room to where Carmela had been sleeping.

As he expected, he found Mrs. Humphries wringing her hands.

"I'm glad you've come, Your Lordship, that I am! Her Ladyship's never been unpredictable ever since she's stayed here, and I've sent the maids searching everywhere and there's not a room in the house that they haven't looked in for her."

"I cannot understand it!" the Earl exclaimed.

"And Suzy's disappeared as well," Mrs. Humphries went on, "not that I can believe she's with Her Ladyship, being a feckless girl who I were thinking of dismissing anyway."

"Suzy?" the Earl questioned in an indifferent tone.

"Suzy Lane, M'Lord."

The Earl was suddenly very still.

"Did you say Suzy *Lane?*"

"Yes, M'Lord."

"Is she any relation to Arthur Lane, the Estate Accountant?"

"She's his niece, M'Lord," Mrs. Humphries replied. "He asked me to take her into the house, but although she's proved far from satisfactory, I gave her chance after chance, so as not to make trouble, so to speak."

"And you say she too is missing?" the Earl asked.

"Well, Emily, who sleeps with her, tells me that she must have left the room last night after she were asleep. She wasn't there this morning when Emily woke."

The Earl did not wait to hear any more. He hurried downstairs and went to the side-door to inspect the marks of the carriage wheels which Newman informed him over and over again were new.

"The marks was not there, M'Lord, when I walks along here just before dinner for a little 'constitutional' as one might say."

"Yes, yes!" the Earl said. "You are quite sure the marks were not there then?"

"I'm sure of it, M'Lord, being rather observant about such matters, and as Your Lordship can see, the vehicle was drawn by two horses."

The Earl was shown the exact place where Carmela's slipper had been found.

He then sent a few footmen running with a summons to the stables, the gardens, and the woodmen.

About twenty minutes later the men employed near the house were all gathered together outside the front door, where he addressed them.

He told them that Lady Felicity was missing and he wanted them all to search their own parts of the Estate and to make certain no bush or ditch or building was overlooked.

"Does Your Lordship think Her Ladyship might have been kidnapped, M'Lord?" the Head Groom asked.

"That is certainly a possibility," the Earl said briefly.

He was remembering only too clearly how much the Gale relatives had talked about Felicity's fortune, and like Carmela he was aware that all their servants would have known about it. The news would have spread like wild-fire over the Estate and in the villages where they lived.

'Blast the money!' he thought to himself. 'The only thing that matters is that Felicity is safe!'

When he finished giving the men instructions, he swung himself into the saddle of his stallion and set off to search for her himself.

As he went, he felt an urgency to find her which was different from any emotion he had ever known before.

He suddenly had a terror that she might have been hurt, drugged, or injured by those who had carried her away.

Even if they had not hurt her physically, he was well aware how sensitive she was and that mentally anything unpleasant that happened would be a tremendous shock.

"I have to find her, and quickly!" the Earl said aloud.

Without really meaning to, he spurred his horse into a gallop.

Chapter Seven

As the Earl drew in his reins he was feeling hot and his stallion was sweating.

He was now on the very edge of the Estate, and he thought despairingly that if Lane and Matthews had carried Felicity into another County, it would be almost impossible to find her.

All the time he had been searching for her, which was now over four hours, he had been aware that his feelings for her were growing and growing until he knew that she meant something very different in his life from anything he had ever known before.

At the same time, he had an almost uncontrollable impulse to murder the men who had abducted her, and he thought he had been remiss in not having had them convicted for their crimes as soon as he had discovered what was going on.

He looked round him and realised he was in a clearing in the wood in which the trees had been felled.

It suddenly struck him that as it was in connection with the sale of timber that he had first discovered that Matthews was stealing, he might, with his mind working in some twisted manner at an effort at revenge, have brought Felicity here, thinking it was the last place anyone would think of looking for her.

It was as if these thoughts came to him like an inspiration from a source outside himself, and now as he saw that there was a track between the tree-trunks, he urged his horse forward.

He was not really optimistic that this was where Felicity would be. At the same time, he had begun to feel despairingly that it was his last hope.

A few moments later he saw in front of him a heavily constructed wooden hut which he knew had been erected by the wood-cutters.

* * *

Carmela knew when dawn came, because faint streaks of light percolated through the narrow cracks between the tree-trunks with which the hut had been made.

The sound of the birds grew louder and she was conscious of feeling stiff and cold and even more frightened than she had been before.

This was because she was sensible enough to realise that her chances of being found were very slender.

She was sure that the wood in which she was imprisoned was in a part of the Estate that was not visited frequently, and she had to face the fact that she might stay here for a very long time before the searchers, if there were any, found her.

She thought she heard a sound outside that was different from any she had heard before, and instantly she ran to the door, shouting as she did so:

"Help! Help!"

Immediately there was what she knew was the sound of an animal scampering away through the undergrowth, and she knew it was probably a deer which had attracted her attention.

She felt ashamed of the panic in her voice and went back to sit down where she had been all night, trying to calm the tumultuous beating of her heart and the breath that came quickly from between her lips.

"I am frightened!" she confessed to herself. "Very, very frightened!"

The light coming in small streaks through the cracks in the walls grew brighter, but as the hours passed nothing else happened.

Because she had hardly slept during the night, Carmela began to doze from sheer exhaustion.

Then, suddenly and unexpectedly, there was the sound of the bolt being raised on the door, and she sat up, alert and half-fearful for the moment that it mght be Matthews or Lane returning.

Then as the sunlight flooded in she saw the outline of a man, large and broad-shouldered, silhouetted against the trees outside, and she gave a cry of joy that seemed to fill the hut with music.

Then the Earl was beside her, pulling her into his arms.

She held on to him, saying incoherently, her words falling over one another:

"You have . . . found . . . me! You have . . . found me! I . . . prayed that . . . you would . . . come! I was . . . so afraid . . . that I would . . . die before . . . you did."

"I have found you," the Earl said in a strange voice.

Then as tears of relief ran down Carmela's cheeks, his lips came down on hers and he held her mouth captive.

For a moment she was too bemused to think of anything except that he was there.

Then as she felt the pressure of his lips, she felt that everything faded away except for the feeling that she was safe, he was holding her close, and she loved him.

His kiss became more demanding, more insistent, and she felt as if he carried her up to the sun and her fears and terror were left behind, and there was only him, the closeness of his arms, and the pressure of his lips.

Then she felt as if the golden rays of sunlight seeped through her body, rising through her breasts and into her throat and up to her lips. The glory of it was his, too, and her love reached towards his heart.

The Earl's arms tightened, then he was kissing the tears from her cheeks, her eyes, her forehead, and again her lips, as she leant against him with a rapture that aroused feelings in her which she had never known before.

Only when she felt as though they had reached the zenith of ecstasy and it was too intense and too wonderful to be borne did Carmela with a little murmur hide her face against the Earl's neck.

But she was still holding on to him as if she was afraid that he might vanish and she would be left alone again.

"How could I have lost you?" the Earl asked in a voice that sounded hoarse and a little unsteady.

"I . . . I was afraid . . . you would . . . never find . . . me."

"I have found you, and I will never let this happen again!"

He put his fingers under her chin to turn her face up to his.

"I have been frantic, desperate!" he said almost as if he spoke to himself.

Then before she could answer he was kissing her, kissing her with slow, passionate kisses which made her feel as if her whole body merged with his and she was no longer herself but part of him.

Finally, when the rapture of his lips made her feel she must have died in the night and was in Heaven, the Earl said:

"I must take you home."

She lifted her head and said incoherently:

"I . . . love you! I . . . tried to call . . . you in the night and tell you . . . where I was . . . but I was . . . afraid that you . . . would not . . . hear me."

"I was awake, thinking about you," the Earl said, "and although it took me a little time to get your message, I am here now, and that is all that matters."

As if Carmela was suddenly aware that she had told the Earl she loved him and that he had kissed her, and they were both things that should not have happened, she moved from his arms, and he said:

"You told me you loved me, my darling, and I knew when I was searching for you that I not only loved you but could not live without you."

Carmela looked at him wide-eyed, and he said:

"We may be first cousins, but that is immaterial beside the fact that you are mine, and I will never let you go."

It was then that Carmela came back to reality, knowing that she would have to tell him the truth but that it was impossible to do so at this moment.

Because she suddenly felt weak, she put her head on his shoulder and frantically tried to think what she should do and how she could tell him that she had been deceiving him and acting a lie.

For the moment nothing seemed real except that she was close to him and he had said that he loved her.

The Earl picked her up in his arms.

"When you were missing," he said, "like 'Cinderella,' you left behind one of your slippers. I knew then that something terrible had happened to you."

"But you did not . . . know who had . . . taken me . . . away," Carmela asked in a low voice, "and carried me here into the . . . wood?"

"When I knew that Lane's niece had also disappeared," the Earl replied, "I was aware of what had happened. But we will talk of it later. You have been through enough for now. I must get you home."

As he spoke he lifted her onto the stallion's back, then untied the reins, which he had attached to a fallen tree.

He mounted behind Carmela, pulled her close against him, and started to ride back through the wood to the clearing.

Carmela shut her eyes.

For the moment she only wanted to think that she was safe and close to the Earl, and that she would confess her deception to him later, when she was feeling stronger.

When they neared the house the Earl asked:

"Did Matthews and Lane say what they were going to do about you? Did they intend to demand a ransom?"

"No," Carmela replied. "They made me sign a cheque for ten thousand pounds and also a letter to Coutts Bank saying they should cash it."

"Ten thousand pounds!" the Earl murmured.

"They said that as soon as they had it they were going abroad."

"I would have them brought to trial if I thought it was worth trying to do so," the Earl said, "but they are the type of criminals who will hang themselves sooner or later, and I would pay a thousand times more to have you safe."

His arms tightened, and as Carmela looked up at him she knew that he wanted to kiss her, but they were now in sight of the house.

Only when the Earl carried her up the stairs to her bedroom, and the servants were all fussing over her because she had come back safely, did she feel that she was once again confronted by her lies.

Sooner or later she would have to explain them to the Earl, and she shivered because she was afraid of his anger.

The Earl was conscious of it.

"Are you cold?" he asked.

"No . . . no! Only . . . happy to be . . . back," Carmela said quickly.

"As I am happy to have you," he said in a low voice.

He carried her into her bedroom and put her down on the bed.

"Put Her Ladyship to bed," he said to Mrs.

Humphries, who was clucking like an agitated hen. "Give her something to eat and let her sleep."

"Yes, M'Lord, of course, M'Lord," Mrs. Humphries replied, "and it's glad and thankful I am that Her Ladyship's returned safe and sound."

The Earl stared down at Carmela lying against the pillows, and there was a look on his face she had never seen before.

"We will talk later," he said quietly.

As he went from the room she wanted desperately to hold on to him to prevent him from leaving her.

Carmela slept, ate, and slept again. But after tea she insisted that she would get up for dinner.

"His Lordship said you were not to do so unless Your Ladyship really felt well enough," Mrs. Humphries argued.

"I am perfectly all right."

She knew she was still a little tired, but at the same time she could not stay away from the Earl any longer. She wanted to be near him, she wanted to talk to him, and she wanted him to kiss her again.

She felt a thrill run through her every time she thought of the wonderful, magical kisses he had given her in the hut, and how she felt he had taken not only her heart but her soul from her body and made them his.

Then insidiously the thought came to her that when he knew the truth, he would not forgive her for pretending to be Felicity!

Perhaps he would be so angry that his love would die and she would never know it again.

She was so frightened that this would happen that she prayed fervently all the time she was dressing, and tried to reassure herself with the thought that she did not have to tell him the truth yet.

Felicity was not yet married, and therefore she could go on pretending to be her until the moment came when she could pretend no longer.

Even though she loved the Earl, her loyalty was still to Felicity, and she must keep her promise and continue to take her place until Jimmy's wife was dead.

Because she was torn between telling the truth to the man she loved and living for the moment with him in a "Fools's Paradise," she could not make up her mind which she wanted most.

Then she knew that if in his anger the Earl sent her away, life without him would be utterly and completely dark and pointless, and she would never again know any happiness.

"I love him! I love him! I love him!" she said on every step of the stairs as she went down to the Salon.

As she went in through the door and saw him standing at the end of the room in front of the mantelpiece, she stood still, thinking how handsome and magnificent he looked in his evening-clothes.

There was a smile on his lips, and as their eyes met the Earl held out his arms and she ran towards him with a little cry of happiness.

His arms encircled her, then he was kissing her, and his kisses were passionate and demanding, as if he had been frustrated in waiting so long until he could give them to her.

"I love you!" he said in a deep voice. "Now tell me what you told me this morning."

"I love . . . you!" Carmela said. "How could I . . . help it?"

"I have no wish for you to help it."

Then he was kissing her again.

Only when the Butler came in to announce that dinner was ready did they draw apart from each other.

When the Earl gave Carmela his arm and she put her hand on it, he covered it with his hand and felt her quiver at his touch.

He smiled at her, and somehow there was no need for words; they each knew what the other was feeling.

At dinner their lips said one thing and their eyes

said another, and Carmela felt as if they were enveloped with a celestial light that came from the sky.

When the meal was over they walked back together to the Salon, and as she sat down on the sofa the Earl said:

"Now we have to make plans, my darling."

She was just about to reply that he should leave it until tomorrow when she could think more clearly, then the door opened and Newman came in with a silver salver in his hand.

"What is it, Newman?" the Earl asked in a tone that told Carmela he did not wish to be disturbed.

"The horses have just returned from Dover, M'Lord," Newman replied, "and the coachman brought with him this letter from His Royal Highness, which he wrote as soon as he boarded the yacht."

The Earl took the letter from the salver, and as the Butler left the room he started to open it, saying as he did so:

"I am afraid our Royal friend will have to look elsewhere for a wife. I am sure together we can find him one."

There was a little pause. Then Carmela said hesitatingly:

"I . . . I do not . . . think the Prince will . . . mind losing me."

Even as she spoke she realised that the Earl was not listening but was staring down at the letter he held in his hand.

He was silent until because she was nervous Carmela asked:

"What is the matter? What has His Royal Highness . . . said to . . . you?"

"It is extraordinary!" the Earl replied. "I can hardly believe the strange things that happen are not part of a dream."

"What is it?" Carmela asked.

The Earl looked down at the letter in his hand before he said:

"Prince Frederich wrote the letter from the yacht just after he boarded it. He thanks me for my hospitality and says that he is extremely grateful for the use of my horses and my yacht. He sends his regards to you in most fulsome terms."

Carmela listened, puzzled because she could not understand why the Earl seemed to think that what he was saying was strange.

Then he continued:

"There is a post-script, which reads:

> *"As I stepped onto the Quay I met one of the Officials of our Embassy in London. He had just returned from Paris, and he handed me a newspaper, saying he had bought it that morning. I am sure the extract I am enclosing will surprise you as much as it surprised me!'"*

"An . . . extract?" Carmela enquired.

In answer the Earl handed her a small piece of newspaper, and as she took it she knew what she would read before she actually did so.

For a moment the news-print seemed to dance in front of her eyes. Then she translated swiftly:

> *"'Lord Salwick, a British Peer, was married yesterday at the British Embassy Church in the Rue du Faubourg St. Honoré to Lady Felicity Gale, daughter of the 6th Earl of Galeston. The happy couple are starting their honeymoon by staying at the Hotel de Fontain- bleu in the Champs Elysées.'"*

Carmela read it to the end and knew as she did so that her hands were trembling.

Then without looking at the Earl she said in a frightened, breathless little voice:

"Forgive me . . . please forgive me . . . I was . . . going to . . . tell you . . . when it was . . . safe for me to do so."

"Are you saying that what is written in the newspaper is true?" the Earl asked incredulously.

Carmela could not reply and after a moment he asked:

"If you are not my cousin Felicity, then who are you?"

"I . . . I am her . . . friend . . . Carmela Lyndon."

The Earl rose to his feet to stand with his back to the mantelpiece, and she felt as if he towered over her.

"I am . . . sorry . . . so very . . . very sorry," she whispered, "but Felicity . . . was . . . in love with . . . Lord Salwick . . . and had been for . . . years."

"Then why did she not marry him before this?" the Earl asked in a puzzled voice.

"Because . . . His Lordship was . . . already married . . . very unhappily, but his wife was dying."

Although she did not look at him, Carmela thought that the Earl's lips tightened, and she went on:

"I . . . I agreed to come . . . here because it was the . . . only way that Felicity could be with . . . Lord Salwick . . . and . . . anyway . . . she did not want him to know about . . . her fortune."

"Why not?"

The Earl's question was abrupt and harsh. Carmela thought despairingly that he was angry and now she had lost him as Felicity might have lost Jimmy.

She knew he was waiting for her answer and after a moment she said:

"Felicity knew . . . because he was . . . proud, that he would refuse to marry a wife who was . . . so wealthy."

"So she was lying to her future husband as you were lying to me?"

"I . . . kn-know it sounds . . . terrible and . . . very reprehensible," Carmela said, "but they were . . . lies for love."

She drew in her breath before she went on:

"I know you think that . . . lies and deception are . . . always . . . wrong and never . . . excusable, but they are . . . sometimes right when they are used to . . . save somebody from suffering or from losing the . . . person they . . . love."

She spoke desperately, feeling as if she was fighting for everything that mattered to her.

Then, because she thought he did not understand, the tears came into her eyes and as they ran down her cheeks she clasped her hands together and said:

"Please . . . please . . . you may not believe it . . . but I love you with my whole heart . . . and soul . . . and if you send me away . . . I shall never . . . however long I live . . . ever love anybody else."

The Earl's eyes searched her face as if he were looking deep down into her soul.

Then as Carmela waited tensely, feeling as if there was no hope and he would repudiate her, he smiled.

His smile seemed to light the whole Salon and dim the candles.

"So you love me!" he said. "And as I love you, what are we to do about it, Carmela?"

She thought her name on his lips was the loveliest sound she had ever heard!

Because she could not help herself, she sprang to her feet and moved close to him, not touching him, only looking at him, fearful that she had misunderstood what he had said.

"I love you!" he said. "And because you are not my cousin and not my Ward, it actually makes things very much easier."

"Do you . . . mean that . . . do you . . . really mean it?"

"I mean it."

The Earl pulled her roughly against him. Then he was kissing her until the world whirled round them and Carmela's feet were no longer on the ground.

He carried her into the sky and placed the moon in her arms and strung the stars round her neck.

Only when she felt as if they were both part of God Himself did the Earl, holding her so closely that she could hardly breathe, ask:

"Have you any idea, my deceitful darling, how we are going to get out of the mess we are in without a scandal?"

She looked up at him apprehensively, and he explained:

"You are staying here with me unchaperoned, and the relatives you have met will think it extraordinary that you should suddenly be marrying under another name."

"Perhaps I ought to . . . go away . . . after all."

The Earl laughed and his arms tightened round her.

"Do you think I would let you? You will never escape me, my lovely one, and what is more, you will never deceive me or lie to me again. I will make sure of that!"

"I have . . . no wish to do so . . . how could I lie to you . . . when I love you so overwhelmingly?"

"I will make certain I do not give you the opportunity," he said. "At the same time, I think we will both have to tell a few 'lies for love,' as you call them."

He put his lips against her forehead and Carmela knew he was thinking before he said:

"How much do you resemble the real Felicity?"

"We are very alike," Carmela replied, "but of course to look more like her I did my hair in the style she wears, and I am also wearing her clothes."

A thought struck her and she added quickly:

"I have not told you . . . but I have . . . no money, and my father and mother are dead. I had been . . . working in a Vicarage . . . looking after the children of the . . . local Vicar."

Her voice sounded worried and frightened, but the Earl only intensified the pressure of his lips against her skin as he said:

"You will have enough to do in the future, my precious one, looking after our own children, and I have plenty of money without needing yours or my cousin Felicity's."

Carmela gave a little sigh of relief and he went on:

"I have a plan, and I think we must act on it at once."

"What is . . . it?"

The Earl spoke slowly, as if he was thinking aloud as he did so.

"We will leave for Paris first thing in the morning. We will find Felicity and her bridegroom, then we will make sure that not only their marriage is reported in the English newspapers, especially *The London Gazette*, but also our own."

Carmela looked puzzled, and he explained:

"You have just told me that you made yourself look like Felicity. Now I want you to look like your adorable self."

Carmela understood and she asked:

"Do you really think when we . . . return, the Gales will be deceived into thinking I am somebody . . . different? And that Felicity is the person they met before?"

"I think you will find," the Earl said, "that people see what they expect to see, and when you are dressed in Paris and have, my precious, a Parisian *chic*, I think together we can deceive them quite skilfully with 'lies for love.'"

"You are so clever!" Carmela cried. "I am sure that when they see Felicity, they may easily think that it was she they met when they came here yesterday."

"If not, we will convince them," the Earl said firmly. "But what is more important than anything else is that I want you as my wife."

The way he spoke made Carmela blush, and once again she hid her face against his shoulder.

"I want you!" the Earl said. "And I feel as if I have fought a very hard battle to win you."

"But . . . now you are . . . victorious!" Carmela whispered.

The Earl looked down at the love in her eyes, the flush on her cheeks, and her lips trembling a little from the traumatic emotions she had passed through.

Then he said very softly:

"I adore your face, your entrancing little brain, your graceful body, but most of all your love."

"They are all yours," Carmela said, "and everything...else that is...me. Tell me that you forgive me, because I want you to trust me and to know that never...never again will I...lie or...deceive you."

"I know that," the Earl said, "and I do trust you, my alluring one, not only because your honesty and goodness shine from you like a light, but also because I am trusting you with my heart, which I have never given to anybody else."

Carmela gave a little cry.

"It is very precious, very wonderful, and I will treasure it for ever and ever!"

The Earl smiled at the happiness in her voice.

Then he pulled her against him and was kissing her again, kissing her until Carmela knew that everything he said was true, and that he had given her his heart as she had given him hers.

Whatever happened in the future, they would never lose each other because their love was true and would last for all eternity.

ABOUT THE AUTHOR

BARBARA CARTLAND, the world's most famous romantic novelist, who is also an historian, playwright, lecturer, political speaker and television personality, has now written over 300 books.

She has also had many historical works published and has written hour autobiographies as well as the biographies of her mother and that of her brother Ronald Cartland, who was the first Member of Parliament to be killed in W.W. II. This book has a preface by Sir Winston Churchill and has just been republished with an introduction by Sir Arthur Bryant.

Barbara Cartland has sold 200 million books over the world, more than half of these in the U.S.A. She broke the world record in 1975 by writing twenty-three books and the four subsequent years with 20, 21, 23 and 24. In addition her album of love songs has just been published, sung with the Royal Philharmonic Orchestra.

Barbara Cartland, who is a Dame of the Order of St. John of Jerusalem, has championed the cause for old people and founded the first Romany Gypsy Camp in the world.

Barbara Cartland is deeply interested in vitamin therapy and is President of the British National Association for Health. Her book, *The Magic of Honey*, has sold millions all over the world.

She has a magazine, *The World of Romance*, and her Barbara Cartland Romantic World Tours will, in communication with British Airways, carry travelers to England, Egypt, India, France, Germany and Turkey.

Barbara Cartland

The world's bestselling author of romantic fiction. Her stories are always captivating tales of intrigue, adventure and love.

☐ 20234	SHAFT OF SUNLIGHT	$1.95
☐ 20014	GIFT OF THE GODS	$1.95
☐ 20126	AN INNOCENT IN RUSSIA	$1.95
☐ 20013	RIVER OF LOVE	$1.95
☐ 14503	THE LIONESS AND THE LILY	$1.75
☐ 13942	LUCIFER AND THE ANGEL	$1.75
☐ 14084	OLA AND THE SEA WOLF	$1.75
☐ 14133	THE PRUDE AND THE PRODIGAL	$1.75
☐ 13032	PRIDE AND THE POOR PRINCESS	$1.75
☐ 13984	LOVE FOR SALE	$1.75
☐ 14248	THE GODDESS AND THE GAIETY GIRL	$1.75
☐ 14360	SIGNPOST TO LOVE	$1.75
☐ 14361	FROM HELL TO HEAVEN	$1.75
☐ 13985	LOST LAUGHTER	$1.75
☐ 14750	DREAMS DO COME TRUE	$1.95
☐ 14902	WINGED MAGIC	$1.95
☐ 14922	A PORTRAIT OF LOVE	$1.95